HFH

Enjoy eight new titles from Harlequin Presents in August!

Lucy Monroe brings you her next story in the fabulous ROYAL BRIDES series, and look out for Carole Mortimer's second seductive Sicilian in her trilogy THE SICILIANS. Don't miss Miranda Lee's ruthless millionaire, Sarah Morgan's gorgeous Greek tycoon, Trish Morey's Italian boss and Jennie Lucas's forced bride! Plus, be sure to read Kate Hardy's story of passion leading to pregnancy in *One Night, One Baby,* and the fantastic *Taken by the Maverick Millionaire* by Anna Cleary!

We'd love to hear what you think about Presents. E-mail us at Presents@hmb.co.uk or join in the discussions at www.iheartpresents.com and www.sensationalromance.blogspot.com, where you'll also find more information about books and authors!

THE SICILIANS

They seek passion—at any price!

A new series by Carole Mortimer

Sicilian heroes—with revenge in mind and romance in their destinies!

Carole Mortimer

AT THE SICILIAN COUNT'S COMMAND

THE SICILIANS

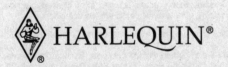

TORONTO • NEW YORK • LONDON
AMSTERDAM • PARIS • SYDNEY • HAMBURG
STOCKHOLM • ATHENS • TOKYO • MILAN • MADRID
PRAGUE • WARSAW • BUDAPEST • AUCKLAND

ISBN-13: 978-0-373-23514-8
ISBN-10:   0-373-23514-3

AT THE SICILIAN COUNT'S COMMAND

First North American Publication 2008.

www.eHarlequin.com

Printed in U.S.A.

All about the author...
Carole Mortimer

CAROLE MORTIMER is one of Harlequin's most popular and prolific authors. Since her first novel was published in 1979, this British writer has shown no signs of slowing her pace. In fact, she has published more than 125 books to date!

Carole was born in a village in England that she claims was so small "if you blinked as you drove through it you could miss seeing it completely!" She adds that her parents still live in the house where she was born, and her two brothers live very close by.

Carole's early ambition to become a nurse came to an abrupt end after only one year of training, due to a weakness in her back, suffered after a fall. Instead, she went on to work in the computer department of a well-known stationery company.

During her time there, Carole made her first attempt at writing a novel for Harlequin. "The manuscript was far too short and the plotline not up to standard, so I naturally received a rejection slip," she says. "Not taking rejection well, I went off in a sulk for two years before deciding to have another go." Her second manuscript was accepted, beginning a long and fruitful career. She says she has "enjoyed every moment of it!"

Carole lives "in a most beautiful part of Britain" with her husband and children.

"I really do enjoy my writing, and have every intention of continuing to do so for another twenty years!"

CHAPTER ONE

'I'M AFRAID I had an ulterior motive for inviting you here this weekend, Wolf— Ah, I believe I hear Angel now,' Stephen Foxwood, Wolf's friend and overnight host, murmured happily, as the sound of a door closing could be heard inside the manor house behind them. The two men were seated outside on the terrace on this warm summer's evening, enjoying a glass of wine before dinner. 'Later,' Stephen promised as he got to his feet. 'Come and meet my—come and meet Angelica Harper,' he corrected as he stood up to enter the sitting room via French windows.

Wolf followed, intrigued. The two men had been friends for several years, and he had believed this Saturday night stay at Stephen's country estate was to discuss the successful conclusion of a joint business deal they had agreed earlier in the week. Stephen certainly hadn't given any indication before now that there was something else he needed to talk about. Or that his current mistress—Angel?—would also be present!

Stephen, as Wolf well knew, had been married to Grace for over thirty years until her death a year ago—not a particularly happy marriage, but not an unhappy one, either. Having a wife certainly hadn't curtailed Stephen's other liaisons; it had just meant that he'd kept those relationships discreetly in the background.

Now that Grace was dead, obviously Stephen didn't feel he had to keep his mistresses a secret any more!

Although Wolf wasn't quite prepared for the appearance of Stephen's latest love. Lowering guarded lids over piercingly dark eyes, he watched the older man cross the room to warmly kiss the cheek of the woman who had entered the sitting room. Years of practice at shielding his thoughts in the boardroom, as well as in the bedroom, allowed Wolf to maintain a bland expression even as he felt shockwaves rock through him while he looked at the woman with whom the usually cynical Stephen was obviously deeply infatuated.

Aged, at most, in her mid-twenties, Angelica Harper had to be at least thirty years younger than Stephen—and she was also the most beautiful woman Wolf had ever set eyes on!

Having been one of the most eligible bachelors in Europe for at least half of his thirty-six years, Wolf had seen—and known intimately—many beautiful women.

But Angelica Harper—five feet eight inches tall, with waist-length black hair, misty grey eyes surrounded by long thick lashes set in a delicately beautiful heart-shaped face, and with the slenderness of her body shown to advantage in her clinging black off-the-shoulder gown—exuded a sensuality that Wolf was totally aware of.

'Come and say hello to Angel, Wolf,' Stephen encouraged, his arm resting possessively on her slender shoulders as he brought her further into the room.

'Angelica,' she corrected dryly as she held out a graceful hand. 'Only Stephen calls me Angel,' she added huskily.

Wolf took that hand automatically, feeling a tingling in his fingers just from touching her. 'Angelica,' he acknowledged guardedly, more than a little disturbed by his immediate awareness of this stunning woman.

Stephen's country estate was thirty miles from London, set in glorious English countryside, and Wolf had come here with the intention of relaxing after the intensity of concluding the business deal he and Stephen had made. The two of them had purchased some land together in the Florida Keys, with the intention of turning it into a development of exclusive villas along with a golf course. Hopefully the resort was destined to become one more of the many successful enterprises that had made Wolf and Stephen two of the richest men in Europe.

But Wolf certainly hadn't expected to meet Stephen's newest young and beautiful mistress while he was here.

And then he recalled that Stephen had casually mentioned there was an ulterior motive to his weekend invitation...

Which had to be meeting this woman, who allowed only her lover to call her Angel.

A woman who made Wolf's body harden in anticipation just looking at her!

'This is Wolf—Count Gambrelli—Angel,' Stephen told her lightly, his blue gaze warm as he introduced the two of them. He was still a handsome man, despite his fifty-eight years. His dark hair having silvered only at the temples, and his body was still lithe and slim in his black evening suit.

'Count Gambrelli.' Angelica nodded a greeting, her eyes widening slightly when the Count didn't let go of her hand after their introduction but continued to hold it in his firm grip long after politeness dictated he should have released her.

She'd heard of Count Carlo—Wolf Gambrelli—of course. An Italian playboy whom the press enjoyed writing about, both on a personal and professional level, his success in business was only circumvented by his prowess with women, which had long ago earned him the nickname of 'Wolf'—a name he seemed to have made entirely his own!

Looking at him, his reputation as a consummate womaniser wasn't too difficult to believe: Wolf Gambrelli was one of the most lethally attractive men Angelica had ever seen.

His shoulder-length hair was a rich burnished gold, rather than the darker colouring she would have expected in a Sicilian. But his skin was a rich mahogany, his eyes a deep, unfathomable brown, and his high cheekbones jutted either side of a patrician nose under which his mouth sat, full and sensuous, above a squarely determined chin. Tall and elegant in a black tie and tuxedo and a snowy-white dress shirt, his outer sophisticated trappings did little to hide the leanly powerful body beneath: wide shoulders, tapered waist, and long, long legs.

Yes, Wolf Gambrelli was a lethally attractive man. But even on a few minutes' acquaintance Angelica detected that he was also a man all too aware of his own power, and that he emanated a ruthlessness which indicated he wouldn't hesitate to use his looks or his wealth to get what—or who—he wanted.

'Please call me Wolf,' he invited softly.

Angelica made a point of releasing her hand even as she gave him a coolly dismissive smile.

It was a coolness that aroused a desire in Wolf to peel her black dress from her temptingly curvaceous body and lay her down on the carpet, to caress and kiss her until she was wanton in his arms!

But at the same time Wolf knew that Stephen's possessive male arm about her slender shoulders was a warning to him that Angelica Harper was Stephen's exclusive property…

Wolf studied Angelica Harper from between narrowed lids. Why was such a young and beautiful woman involved with a man so much her senior? For his money? Now that Stephen was widowed, was she hoping to become one of those trophy wives? A woman who traded on her youth and beauty in order to trap herself a rich husband? Stephen certainly looked besotted enough to offer her that!

'Drink, Angel?' Stephen asked.

'That would be lovely, thank you,' Angelica Harper accepted huskily. 'Is this a long or short visit to England, Wolf?' she turned to enquire politely, once Stephen had crossed the room to pour her a glass of chilled white wine from the bottle the butler had brought in earlier.

'I haven't decided yet,' Wolf found himself replying, his attention caught and held by the peachy-pearl fullness of Angelica Harper's lips.

Lips that were surely made for kissing and being kissed...!

'Here we are.' Stephen's smile included both Wolf and Angelica as he returned with the glass of wine, handing it to her before once again draping his arm lightly about her shoulders. 'You're looking exceptionally lovely this evening, Angel,' he complimented, his blue eyes warmly appreciative. 'Don't you think so, Wolf?' he prompted proudly.

Wolf's mouth tightened as he noted the delicate blush that had entered Angelica's creamy cheeks. This woman was undoubtedly beautiful—mesmerisingly so. But the fact that she obviously belonged exclusively to another man made null and void the primitive urge Wolf had to claim Angelica for his own!

'Angelica is very beautiful,' he acknowledged non-commitally, none of his inner turmoil visible.

What was wrong with him?

He had seen and physically known dozens of beautiful women. Blonde, brunettes, redheads. Other women with hair as ebony as Angelica Harper's. So what was it about this particular woman that made him want to fling Stephen's arm from her shoulders and throw her over his own shoulder, to carry her off like some marauding Viking?

Just imagining the things he would like to do to her once he had carried her off made his body pulse hotly!

Angelica gave Stephen a questioning look from beneath lowered lashes, knowing him too well by now to be fooled by the lightness of his tone, and aware that there was some sort of purpose behind Wolf Gambrelli being here with them this weekend. After months of sharing a home with Stephen at weekends, whenever their mutual commitments allowed, she knew that he rarely did or said anything that didn't have a purpose or ulterior motive.

Quite what purpose there was behind Wolf Gambrelli's visit here, she as yet had no idea!

Although she did find the intensity of Wolf Gambrelli's dark gaze more than a little unnerving. His first searing appraisal of her had felt as if he had stripped her dress from her body and gazed his fill of her nakedness—something that made her feel hot all over.

Which was ridiculous!

Wolf Gambrelli was a Sicilian playboy of such repute that there wasn't a month that went by without one glossy magazine or another featuring a couple of pages of photo spreads of his latest relationship. The man seemed to change his women as often as he changed the silk sheets reputed to be on his bed!

All of which proved he was exactly the type of man Angelica had absolutely no intention of being attracted to!

'I believe it's time for us to go in to dinner,' she said with some relief as she saw Holmes, Stephen's butler, hovering in the doorway.

Coming from an ordinary home, which she'd shared with her parents and two younger sisters, and then having shared a flat with three other girls while at university, she still found the opulence of Stephen's lifestyle a little over-whelming at times—felt she would have just liked to cook the two of them a meal occasionally, which they would eat at the kitchen table. But that was something that Stephen had assured her was a definite no-no; the kitchen and servants' quarters in both his London and his country home were completely off-limits to her.

'Perhaps you would like to escort Angel into dinner, Wolf…?' Stephen suggested as he removed his arm from her shoulders. 'Much as I would like to, I appreciate I can't keep her all to myself,' he added huskily.

'Certainly,' the Sicilian Count moved obligingly to her side, holding out his arm invitingly.

Angelica shot Stephen another questioning look before placing her hand lightly on Wolf Gambrelli's arm, aware of the hardness beneath her fingers, like tempered steel beneath silk, as he moved with the grace of a natural athlete.

Although quite when this man found the time, between the bedroom and the boardroom, to hone his body to such muscled perfection, she couldn't imagine!

She removed her hand from his arm as quickly as possible when they reached the dining room— although her relief was short-lived as he moved to pull her chair back for her to sit down. His silky blond hair brushed lightly against her bare shoulder as he bent down to push the chair in behind her, the slightly elusive smell of his cologne invading her senses as she felt the warmth of his breath dangerously close to her earlobe.

Angelica moved sharply away from his slightly overwhelming proximity, at the same time frowning her irritation; there had surely been no reason for him to get quite that close!

'It's high time that we began to entertain, Angel,' Stephen said once Angelica was seated between the two men at the round table.

Angelica frowned slightly. In the six months since she had begun to spend some of her weekends with Stephen they had never entertained, having spent the majority of that time getting to know each other. Wolf Gambrelli was their first dinner guest, let alone weekend guest...

'I really must start to show you off rather than greedily keeping you to myself,' Stephen added lightly. 'Don't you think so, Wolf?'

Angelica looked at Wolf Gambrelli from beneath lowered lashes as he took his time answering the older man, his expression as unreadable as Angelica's own.

'I'm not sure I would want to share her with anyone else, either, if she were mine,' Wolf finally answered tautly, knowing that if Angelica Harper really *were* his, he would definitely want to greedily keep her to himself!

Perhaps that was the reason for this inexplicable attraction? Perhaps it was the fact that

Angelica Harper wasn't his, that she was so obviously Stephen's, and the fact that she wasn't available, that made her more desirable in his eyes?

No, that couldn't be it, he instantly dismissed; he had always made a point of never poaching on another man's marriage or a prior claim to a woman. The newspapers might like to depict him as an international playboy, but that didn't mean he didn't have a moral code that he lived by.

Unfortunately, just looking at Angelica Harper, gazing into the deep mystery of those misty grey eyes, lowering his gaze to the bare skin of her shoulders and the firm thrust of her breasts against the soft material of her dress, was enough to make him want to throw his moral code out of the window along with his senses!

Stephen gave a husky laugh. 'That's honest, anyway!'

Honesty had nothing to do with it; Wolf knew himself well, and he was truly intrigued by the beautiful Angelica Harper!

Though he knew nothing about her apart from the fact that she was the most breathtakingly beautiful and sensually arousing woman he had ever met.

And that she belonged to Stephen…

'Stop teasing Count Gambrelli, Stephen,' Angelica told him shortly, her grey eyes flashing a warning as he raised innocent brows. The look she gave him in return promised there would be a reckoning later. 'I hope that you like smoked salmon, Count…?' She turned to Wolf politely.

Although his heated gaze—as dark and warm as melted chocolate—showed no such politeness as it rested hungrily on her slightly parted lips, completely taking her breath away. Even as her tongue instinctively moved to moisten the lips he stared at so intently, that dark gaze followed the movement of her tongue before rising again to meet hers in a look that seared.

'More wine, Wolf?' Stephen lightly broke into the tension, and Angelica looked up to find Holmes standing patiently beside their guest, waiting to replenish his glass with the white wine that was to accompany their first course.

Angelica sucked air into her starved lungs as Wolf Gambrelli slowly broke their locked gaze to turn and nod his head abruptly to the butler, his jaw so tightly clenched it was possible to see a nerve pulsing there. His high cheekbones were clearly visible, and those dark eyes were guarded as he raised his wine glass and swallowed deeply.

He was reacting to Angelica Harper's sensual beauty like a man deprived of water in a desert, Wolf recognised self-disgustedly!

But it was more obvious than ever, after Stephen's flattering remarks to her just now, that Wolf's assumption that the other man was totally besotted with Angelica Harper had been correct. And no amount of desire, of wanting her on Wolf's part, looked likely to change that.

He began to eat his smoked salmon, not tasting the succulent delicacy as he realised he had lost his appetite. His appetite for food, at least! He hadn't been aroused just looking at a woman since he was an inexperienced teenager!

'Angelica is an—unusual name,' he remarked lightly.

She nodded. 'My mother has always been very keen on plants, herbs and flowers—I have twin sisters at home called Saffron and Rosemary,' she added ruefully. 'Goodness knows what my mother would have named us if we had been boys—Basil, Bennet and Comfrey, perhaps!' She gave a huskily dismissive laugh.

The throaty sound of her laughter slid so sensually over Wolf's flesh it felt almost like a caress, making the hair rise on the back of his neck and heat course through his veins.

'Your mother is obviously a wise and far-seeing woman,' Stephen put in huskily. 'Angel is a perfect name for you, my love,' he told her warmly, one of his hands moving briefly to cover hers.

'I think you may be biased,' she told the older man affectionately.

Wolf really wasn't sure he was going to be able to take a whole evening—let alone an overnight stay—of this! If Stephen was any more besotted with his exotically beautiful 'Angel', he would be drooling at the mouth!

It wasn't comforting to know that Wolf wanted to drool right along with him!

Angelica Harper, as if sensing Wolf's hooded gaze on her, turned to include him in the conversation. 'Which part of Italy do you come from, Count Gambrelli?' she prompted politely.

He didn't want politeness from this woman, Wolf recognised, as he inwardly brooded. In fact, his instincts where Angel was concerned were all completely primitive!

But at least the conversation became more general after that, as the three of them discussed the merits, or otherwise, of the different places they had visited in the world.

And Wolf did learn more, bit by bit, about the mysterious Angelica Harper as the evening progressed.

Before she had met Stephen, a year ago, her life

seemed to have been one of being brought up in
a close-knit family in Kent, followed by three
years at university obtaining a degree in politics,
and then moving on to a job in London as assis-
tant to an aide to an elected politician—something she obviously enjoyed if the enthusiasm in
her voice as she talked of it was anything to go by.

Which all sounded so at odds with the trophy
girlfriend thing, or the potential trophy wife Wolf
had assumed her to be…

'You must miss all that now…?' he enquired
interestedly, lounging back in his chair as the three
of them lingered at the dining table, drinking
coffee at the end of the meal.

Angelica gave Wolf Gambrelli a frowning look.
'Why would I miss it…?'

She had sensed Wolf Gambrelli's critical gaze
on her more than once as they ate dinner, and had
chosen to ignore it and him—although, in truth,
it was virtually impossible to ignore a man as sensually attractive as Wolf Gambrelli!

He shrugged those broad shoulders. 'Leaving
London and your job—'

'But I haven't left London. Or given up my job.
Why would I…?' Angelica looked at him questioningly, completely mystified as to why he
should have assumed that she had.

'Much as I would like to keep Angel with me all the time, Wolf, she prefers to remain an independent woman,' Stephen told the younger man as he smiled proudly at Angelica. 'Despite all my urgings for her to let me look after her and cosset her, she absolutely refuses to give up her own apartment or her job.'

'Well, of course I do!' Angelica exclaimed. 'I love having my own apartment. And my job. Besides, I would be bored out of my mind if I stayed at home all day doing nothing!'

'You see, Wolf—' Stephen laughed softly '—Angel is a rare find—a truly independent as well as a beautiful woman!'

A rare find indeed, Wolf acknowledged frowningly. His assumption that Angelica Harper had moved in with Stephen and now lived off him in return for sharing his bed had proved to be totally incorrect.

Which only succeeded in deepening the air of mystery that surrounded her...

For her part, Angelica found Wolf Gambrelli's assumption that she had given up her independence when she'd met Stephen extremely offensive.

For one thing, after living with two sisters and then sharing a house with three other girls while at university, it was lovely to at last have some space of her own. And she enjoyed her job far too much to even think about giving it up.

Just because she stayed with Stephen some weekends, it didn't mean she had to be kept by him, too.

'You've been a charming and attentive hostess this evening, darling. Thank you.' The warmth of Stephen's smile took away some of the sting of Wolf Gambrelli's recent conversation.

'You're welcome.' Angelica returned his smile, relieved that the evening was obviously coming to an end. 'I think I'll go up to bed now—if no one minds…?'

'Not at all, darling,' Stephen assured her. 'I could do with an early night myself.'

She instantly frowned her concern. 'Are you—?'

'I'm fine, Angel. Just a little tired, that's all,' Stephen dismissed easily. 'I hope you don't mind the two of us making an early night of it, Wolf?' he added ruefully to the other man.

Wolf's elbows were resting on the table-top, his laced fingers having clenched tightly together as he listened to their conversation. At the same time he knew it was utterly ridiculous for him to take exception to the fact that Stephen and Angelica obviously couldn't wait to be alone together.

Even if the vivid images that thought brought

to his own mind were guaranteed to ensure that Wolf's own night would be a sleepless one!

'I'm not as young as I thought I was,' Stephen added wryly.

'None of us are,' Wolf bit out tautly, sure that sharing a bed with the beautiful and sensuous Angelica couldn't be in the least restful.

'Goodnight, Wolf,' Angelica murmured as she stood up. 'I hope you sleep well.'

His eyes narrowed with suspicion as he searched the beauty of her face for some sign of mockery—some indication that she knew there was no way he was going to sleep at all tonight, when his mind would be full of images of her long silky legs wrapped around another man's body as he took her to the heights of ecstasy.

Those misty grey eyes returned his gaze with steady regard, giving away none of Angelica Harper's inner thoughts, and he could find no sign of mockery in the polite smile that curved the sensuality of her lips.

Which wasn't to say there wasn't any—Angelica Harper might just be a consummate actress!

'I'm sure that I shall,' he returned dryly. 'It has been a—pleasure meeting you, Angelica,' he added throatily, before he could stop himself.

She continued to look at him keenly for several

seconds, before giving a slight inclination of her head. 'Thank you. Coming, Stephen…?' She turned to invite softly.

'I'll be right behind you,' he promised warmly.

Wolf's gaze remained intently on Angelica as he watched her leave, her long dark hair moving silkily down the length of her spine, emphasising the soft curve of her bottom as her hips moved gracefully, her legs smooth and shapely…

'How much of a pleasure *was* it meeting Angel, Wolf…?' Stephen murmured.

Wolf's gaze returned sharply to the older man as Angelica closed the dining room door softly behind her, taking most of the warmth in the room with her. Wolf immediately masked his expression as he saw the searching curiosity in Stephen's eyes.

'As you said earlier, Stephen, Angelica is very beautiful,' he replied tersely. 'Where on earth did you find her?' he prompted conversationally.

The older man shrugged. 'I didn't find her. She found me,' he explained ruefully. 'My lucky day, hmm?' he added.

'Indeed,' Wolf acknowledged noncommittally.

'I had better go up now, otherwise Angel will only worry,' Stephen told him with an affectionate grimace. 'But we'll talk tomorrow, Wolf?'

Wolf's brows quirked. 'About your ulterior

motive for inviting me here, perhaps…?' he said speculatively, knowing he was no more in the mood for a business discussion *now* than Stephen obviously was.

Having always put his business life first and his personal life second, Wolf was very aware that his mind had been full of thoughts of Angelica Harper this evening—that images of her in Stephen's bed later this evening had kept intruding. As they still were!

Did she sleep naked? Or did she perhaps wear something satiny and alluring with which to tempt her ageing lover?

Just thinking of that long swathe of silky dark hair being the only covering to those uptilted breasts, leaving her slender waist and curvaceous thighs bare, was enough to drive every other thought from Wolf's mind.

'Yes,' Stephen confirmed with a sigh, now looking as weary as he had claimed he felt. 'I'm sorry to keep putting it off like this, but I—' He shook his head. 'We'll talk tomorrow,' he promised.

Wolf was too restless to even bother undressing when he reached his own room a few minutes later, let alone attempting to go to bed, and decided to go back downstairs to the library and pour himself a glass of the brandy he would find in a decanter there. He might even get a little drunk. Anything to stop him from thinking of Angelica Harper in Stephen's bed.

Not very likely, he acknowledged grimly as, quietly leaving his bedroom, he saw Angelica leaving a bedroom further down the hallway. Stephen's bedroom? Wolf wondered as he stood transfixed. If so, she hadn't stayed long with her lover, both men having come upstairs only ten minutes or so ago.

He had an almost immediate answer to his curiosity as Angelica, wearing a pale grey silk wrap that clung to the curves of her stunning body, paused outside a bedroom door across the hallway from the one she had just left, knocking softly.

Stephen opened the door almost instantly at the sound of that knock, had Angelica slipped past him into the bedroom before Stephen closed the door behind her.

Wolf's breath left his lungs in a shaky sigh as he leant back against the wall, instantly tormented by thoughts of what was happening in Stephen's bedroom, of Angelica in the other man's arms.

And he knew that, brandy or not, there wasn't a hope in hell that he would be able to sleep tonight!

CHAPTER TWO

'AND to think I had stopped believing in mermaids long ago!'

Angelica gave a surprised start at the sound of that taunting voice—that familiar taunting voice. She instantly moved to tread water so she could turn and look at Wolf Gambrelli, who was standing by the edge of the swimming pool, looking down at her with broodingly dark eyes.

The luxury of having Stephen's indoor pool to come down to at six-thirty in the morning had been one she hadn't been able to resist when she's begun staying here with him. An early-morning swim was part of her weekend daily routine now.

A swim that had always remained solitary until today. Stephen was usually already busy in his study at this time of the day, dealing with any e-mails or faxes that might have come in over-night.

The fact that she was only wearing a red bikini and her hair was slicked back wetly from her makeupless face after swimming her usual fifty lengths of the pool only increased her feelings of disadvantage. Wolf Gambrelli was dressed in a short-sleeved black shirt and tailored black trousers that did nothing to hide the powerful width of his shoulders, his tapered waist and long legs.

'Count Gambrelli,' she greeted politely.

'Angel,' he returned, the expression in those dark brown eyes unreadable.

Angelica's cheeks flushed slightly at his easy use of Stephen's name for her. 'If you're looking for Stephen—'

'I'm not,' he rasped dismissively.

Then what was he doing here? The fact that he was fully dressed didn't seemed to indicate he had come down for a swim…

'Breakfast is being served in the dining room if you're—'

'I'm not hungry, either, Angel,' Wolf Gambrelli interrupted, coming down on his haunches at the poolside to hold out a hand to her. 'At least, not for food…' he added enigmatically.

Angelica frowned as she looked at that hand: his fingers were long and tapered. She wasn't sure she wanted to get out of the water and reveal herself in her skimpy bikini—and she was *very* sure she didn't want to put her hand in Wolf Gambrelli's!

Which was pretty ridiculous; all she had to do was remember that Wolf Gambrelli was exactly the sort of man she had no intention of ever being attracted to, and that should be enough to completely nullify these feelings of physical awareness.

She reached out and took his hand, and noticed the muscles moving in his shoulders as he pulled her effortlessly out of the water to stand beside him.

Too close beside him, she instantly realised, her breath catching in her throat as his deep brown eyes darkened appreciatively and his gaze moved slowly down the length of her body, lingering on the creaminess of her breasts before going down to the hollow curve of her stomach and the gentle swell of her hips.

Angelica swallowed hard, knowing that telling herself this man was everything she didn't want in her life—a playboy and a womaniser—hadn't worked. She was so very aware of the heat of his body, of the leashed power in his wide shoulders—of the fact that her own body had become warm from the appreciative caress in his eyes as he unabashedly looked his fill of her.

'If you'll excuse me, I usually have a soak in the hot Jacuzzi after my swim.' She turned abruptly away to pick up her towel from the lounger, wiping the pool water from her face before wrapping the towel toga-style about her body.

'Go ahead,' Wolf drawled, having been unable to resist joining her when he'd returned from strolling in the garden before breakfast and seen Angelica Harper alone in the pool.

Wolf had noted the statuary when he'd entered the warmth of the poolhouse—goddesses, mostly—but none of them compared in beauty to Angelica Harper. He'd stood and watched her swim the length of the pool, her skin alabaster, the beauty of her face unadorned by make-up and dominated by those misty grey eyes surrounded by thick dark lashes.

If anything, completely stripped of any sophisticated adornment, she looked more beautiful this morning than she had last night!

He walked several feet behind her now as, after one more frowning glance up at him, she walked down the poolside to where steam rose invitingly from the ten-foot circular Jacuzzi Wolf had passed on his way in, a cascade of greenery shielding the tub from any prying eyes outside the poolhouse.

Wolf's mouth tightened as he easily imagined Angelica and Stephen lazing naked in the steaming water before getting out and making love together.

In fact, his imagination had been working overtime since he'd first set eyes on Angelica Harper!

As his sleepless night testified, he acknowledged self-derisively.

Not that one sleepless night was a problem. No, it was the fact that he found Angelica Harper just as sensually disturbing this morning as he had last night that was the problem.

Because, after witnessing Angelica going to Stephen's bedroom last night, there was no doubting the intimacy of their relationship!

'Mmm,' Angelica murmured appreciatively as she sank beneath the waves of bubbling water, sitting down on one of the underwater tiled benches and resting her head back against the side to look up at the broodingly silent Wolf Gambrelli. 'You really should go for a swim and then come for a dip in here, Wolf,' she told him brightly as she luxuriated in the Jacuzzi. 'It's absolutely wonderful!'

'I prefer to watch you,' he assured her, and again he got down on his haunches to pick up a strand of the long dark hair she had lifted out of the water and draped over the side.

Bringing him close, Angelica noted nervously. Too dangerously close, she acknowledged, as her breathing suddenly felt constricted, and her gaze was caught and held by the caress of those long fingers on the thick strand of her hair.

'Do you love him?'

She raised startled eyes to Wolf Gambrelli's face. The harshness of his tone was matched by the hard glitter in his dark eyes and the tight clenching of his jaw. 'I beg your pardon?' she replied uncertainly.

His hand tightened on the thick strand of her hair and he twisted it around his long fingers. Repeatedly. So that Angelica was forced to lift her head, which brought her face so close to his she could now see the flecks of gold amongst the brown in his shrewd eyes.

'I asked if you love Stephen,' Wolf Gambrelli repeated. 'Surely that's a simple enough question to answer?' he prompted at her silence. 'Either a yes or no will do,' he added, when she still didn't answer.

Well, no...no, it wouldn't. Her relationship with Stephen was much more complex than that. They were still getting to know each other. And while she might care for Stephen, she wasn't sure she understood the life he had led these last thirty years.

Wolf's jaw clenched as she continued not to reply to his question, his eyes becoming glacial, his hand tightening on the silkiness of her hair. His scrutiny moved down as he caused her throat to arch and her breasts to thrust forward, her hardened nipples clearly outlined against the soft material of the red bikini top.

He knew a sudden hunger to see those breasts bared, to know whether her nipples were a dark, tempting brown or a dusky, inviting pink, to touch and taste them until he heard her throaty groans of pleasure.

'Count Gambrelli, you're hurting me!' Her surprised protest broke into his erotic imaginings.

Wolf frowned darkly as he looked down at her, his frown deepening as he realized he had tightened his hand in her hair and twisted her head back.

He gave a self-disgusted snort as he unravelled that silky tress from his fingers before straightening, thrusting his hands into his trouser pockets as he looked down at her, dark storminess in his eyes now. 'Stephen is obviously besotted with you—'

'I don't believe that is any of your business, Count Gambrelli.'

'I find it…surprising that a young and beautiful woman like you would give herself to a man for his money,' he opined.

Angelica stopped rubbing the sore area of her scalp. '*"Give"* myself?' she repeated slowly.

His mouth twisted derisively. 'I saw you go to Stephen's bedroom last night, so I think it is a little late for you to attempt to play the outraged virgin!'

He had seen her?

'And just *how* did you see me, Count Gambrelli?' she demanded, having not seen him in the hallway the previous night. 'Did you stand in the shadows and spy on us?' she scoffed, and she surged up on a wave of bubbles in the Jacuzzi, then stood up to wade across and climb out of the tub. She grabbed up her towel to wrap it around herself before turning to face him, her cheeks flushed with anger and her eyes glittering with the same emotion. 'Well?' she challenged furiously.

What on earth was he doing? Wolf wondered with inward self disgust.

Had his heated response to this woman's sensual beauty made him forget all discretion?

'No, of course I was not spying on you,' he denied coldly. 'I decided to go back downstairs for a brandy—'

'And by pure coincidence it happened to be at the time I went to Stephen's bedroom?' she concluded. She gave a disgusted shake of her head. 'I don't believe my relationship with Stephen is any of your business, Count Gambrelli.'

'Stephen is my friend—'

'I don't believe friends spy on each other!' Angelica challenged him again.

'I have told you I was not spying—'

'I don't believe you,' she said flatly.

Wolf stiffened at this denial, nostrils flaring. 'Do you really think that I would willingly make myself a witness to Stephen's infatuation with you?' he refuted.

The angry flush deepened in her cheeks. 'Stephen's feelings for me, and mine for him, are absolutely none of your concern—'

'Not even if I believe he is making a fool of himself over a woman young enough to be his daughter?' Wolf came back swiftly.

Angelica became very still, lowering her lashes as a shield to the shock she knew would be in her eyes.

Because, without realising it, Wolf Gambrelli had inadvertently hit on exactly what her relationship was to Stephen. She was his daughter. His illegitimate daughter. Born to Kathleen Singer eight months after her affair with the married Stephen Foxwood had ended.

Angelica had always known that her mother's husband, Neil Harper, wasn't her real father—she had been a precocious five years old when Neil and her mother were married. But it had never mattered. Neil had always treated Angelica exactly the same as his own daughters by Kathleen—Saffron and Rosemary.

Although Kathleen had told Angelica the name of her real father when, aged twelve, she had asked about him, Angelica's curiosity hadn't been strong enough at the time for her to want to trace him. Especially when, at eighteen and a little more curious, she had discovered that Stephen was still married to Grace.

But a year ago she had seen Grace's obituary in the newspaper—had learnt that Stephen and Grace's thirty-year marriage had been childless, which had reawakened Angelica's own curiosity about the father she had never known.

A curiosity she had discussed with her mother and Neil before she had even attempted to see Stephen Foxwood. As she had known they would be, both Neil and Kathleen had been completely supportive of her decision to at least make contact with her real father and let him know that he did have a child after all—a daughter.

That first meeting between father and daughter had been extremely emotional…

It had been followed by further meetings, and by Angelica agreeing six months later to start occasionally staying with Stephen at weekends, so that they could get to know each other better.

They were still getting to know each other…

And now this man—this Wolf Gambrelli, this arrogant Sicilian count—had come along and passed judgement on a relationship he knew absolutely nothing about!

She and Stephen had agreed from the onset that for the foreseeable future their relationship would remain private between the two of them. A secret that Stephen had obviously kept even from his close friend Wolf Gambrelli. Resulting in this supercilious man making assumptions about their relationship—insulting assumptions.

Angelica didn't believe for a moment that Wolf Gambrelli's comments about their assumed relationship were out of concern for Stephen. She had seen the searing way Wolf Gambrelli had watched her every movement last night. And again, this morning, she'd seen the desire in his eyes when he looked at her, and had known that he was pursuing self-interest rather than concern for his friend.

A self-interest that was going nowhere as far as she was concerned. Wolf Gambrelli was just a younger version of Stephen. And while she might forgive Stephen all his past indiscretions—simply because he was her father and she was growing to love him for that alone—she certainly wasn't stupid enough to become involved with a man who was just as emotionally unreliable!

'Do you have nothing to say in your defence?' Wolf Gambrelli broke into the lengthy silence.

Angelica drew in a controlling breath before raising her lids to look at him scornfully. 'I'm not on trial, Count Gambrelli.'

'You are playing with the emotions of a man I consider to be a good friend as well as my business partner—'

'Stephen is a big boy, Count Gambrelli,' she told him firmly. 'I'm sure he doesn't need you to intercede on his behalf!'

'Stephen doesn't seem to see you in the way that I do,' Wolf grated harshly.

She raised one dark, mocking brow. 'And just how is that, Count Gambrelli?'

Wolf's jaw clenched, his frustration with this situation growing. Having spent most of the night thinking of this woman, imagining her naked and wanton in another man's arms, he should never have come in here when he saw her alone in the pool—certainly should never have begun this present conversation.

He was making his own attraction to Angelica far too obvious.

And that wasn't a situation that sat comfortably on his usually self-assured, emotionally self-contained shoulders!

'Admittedly you seem cleverer than most, by keeping your apartment and your job, and maintaining your independence,' Wolf admitted. 'But as that only seems to have made Stephen even more besotted with you, I have no doubt that he will very soon insist that you change that arrangement!'

'Really?' Angelica Harper came back derisively. 'Thank you for sharing that information with me, Count Gambrelli.' She gave a sharp inclination of her head. 'Now, if you will excuse me…? I find the air in here rather—oppressive!'

Wolf wanted to reach out and stop her from leaving. Wanted to grasp both her arms and shake her. Wanted to take her in his arms and kiss her until she agreed to leave Stephen and come to *him*…!

This realisation was shocking, totally at odds with his usual casual and unpossessive attitude towards women, and all he could do was stand and watch as Angelica walked away from him.

No doubt with the intention of telling her 'besotted' lover exactly how he had just insulted her!

Which meant not only had he made his own interest in Angelica obvious, but he had also probably just completely ruined a friendship and business partnership that had existed for years.

But there was no evidence that Angelica had mentioned the incident to Stephen when the three of them sat down to breakfast together an hour later, the older man seeming just as friendly and relaxed as he always was.

Angelica's behaviour towards Wolf was a little frosty—understandably so!—but other than that she gave no indication that their conversation in the poolhouse had ever taken place.

Wolf studied her covertly: her long, silky hair had been washed and dried and pulled back in a ponytail, emphasising her high cheekbones and the delicate line of her jaw. Her only make-up appeared to be a lipgloss that matched the colour of the red tee shirt she wore with faded fitted denims, the swell of her breasts temptingly visible above its low neckline…

'Would you go riding with Angel this morning, Wolf?'

His attention had been so intently focused on Angelica, on those tantalising glimpses of her creamy breasts, that for a moment Wolf found himself completely disorientated, frowning darkly as he turned to Stephen. 'Sorry?' he responded distantly.

Stephen raised silver-grey brows at Wolf's obvious distraction. 'I was suggesting you might like to go for a ride with Angel…?'

That was what he had thought the other man had said! Except he now realised Stephen had been talking about *horses*…!

The line Wolf's thoughts had been following had taken him in another direction entirely!

'Stephen, I really don't think—'

'Oh, come on, Angel.' The older man cut chidingly through her protest. 'Unfortunately I have a conference call to deal with this morning, and you know I don't like you going out alone just yet. Angel has only just learnt to ride,' he explained to Wolf.

But Wolf Gambrelli was the last person Angelica wanted to accompany her anywhere!

A fact Stephen should have been all too aware of after the conversation they'd had before breakfast, when she'd told him that she believed he ought to explain their real relationship to Wolf— that the Sicilan seemed somewhat confused as to her role in Stephen's life.

She could have put it more bluntly than that, but was aware that Wolf Gambrelli had been a close friend of Stephen's for years—that it wasn't up to her to cast a shadow over that friendship. Stephen had assured her that he had every intention of talking to Wolf about their relationship this weekend. Just not yet, it seemed…

'I'm sure Count Gambrelli has better things to do this morning than go riding with me.' She spoke determinedly even as she shot Stephen an appealing glance, not sure she could take any more of Wolf Gambrelli's insulting remarks without retaliating.

Because if she really had been Stephen's latest mistress, then she would have lost no time in telling Wolf Gambrelli exactly what he could do with his very personal remarks!

The one thing she had absolutely insisted on when she'd agreed to spend time with Stephen, so that the two of them could get to know each other better, was that she didn't want anything from him. Not the help with her career that he'd offered, or the money he had wanted to settle on her.

But she would have felt exactly the same way if she had been Stephen's mistress rather than his daughter!

'You don't have anything else to do this morning, do you, Wolf?' Stephen asked.

Something didn't add up here, Wolf decided. For one thing, Stephen didn't seem in the least concerned at the thought of Wolf going off for the morning with Angelica. Obviously Stephen knew him well enough to know of his code concerning attached women, but even so the other man was putting a lot of trust in him...

And Wolf still couldn't work out why Angelica hadn't told her lover about his earlier rudeness to her. It had been the obvious thing for her to do, after all.

'Why not?' he accepted languidly. 'I'm sure I would greatly enjoy riding with Angel,' he added softly, and he saw the delicate colour creep into Angelica's alabaster cheeks at his deliberately provocative reply.

'Great!' Stephen nodded his satisfaction with the arrangement, seeming totally unaware of the undercurrents in the conversation. 'I'll feel much happier knowing Angel is in safe hands.'

Wolf wouldn't have felt so quite so pleased about the arrangement if he were Stephen—not when Wolf's own feelings towards Angelica Harper were far from innocent.

And, more disturbing, far from under his normally rigid control...!

CHAPTER THREE

WOLF felt even less confident about maintaining that control when he joined Angelica down at the stables half an hour later. The figure-hugging jodhpurs she wore left little to the imagination. Even her billowing white shirt, which was tucked into the narrow waistband of those jodhpurs, tantalized—hinting at, rather than hiding, the firm uptilt of her unconfined breasts beneath.

'I hope you aren't expecting too much of me, Count Gambrelli,' she told him ruefully.

Wolf lifted his gaze sharply from the allure of her unfettered breasts, knowing by the way her brows had risen in query that she was aware of his heated appraisal.

'I really am just a novice at this,' she confided, even as the stable-lad cupped his hands so that she could swing herself up onto the back of the placid black mare that had been saddled for her.

He'd been caught staring like an untried youth,

Wolf acknowledged self-disgustedly. What a gauche, unsophisticated fool she made of him!

'All evidence to the contrary—Angel!' he flung back at her as he took the reins of a dapple-grey mount from another stable-lad to swing himself easily up into the saddle.

Angelica realised quickly that what he implied was too explicit to be mistaken for anything other than what it was.

He really was an arrogant bastard, she decided. So damned sure of himself. To the point that she knew she would have no sympathy with him at all once Stephen told him of their true relationship and he was made to look a complete idiot.

In fact, she was so annoyed, so incensed by Wolf Gambrelli's continued rudeness towards her, that she no longer felt any inclination to prevent him from digging himself even further into that particular hole!

The fact that he looked absolutely magnificent, sitting confidently astride the grey, his hair a burnished gold in the sunlight, his white shirt and a pair of Stephen's jodhpurs and black riding boots giving him a raffishly compelling appearance that was breathtaking, did nothing to lessen her feelings of resentment.

Wolf Gambrelli was too damned good-looking

for his own good, and too cavalier when it came to women. Surely he deserved to be taken down a peg or two!

'Thanks, Tom.' She bestowed a grateful smile on the stable-boy as he helped her to put her booted feet into the stirrups. 'Ready, Count?' she prompted dryly as he watched the exchange with narrowed eyes.

As if he suspected her of trying to seduce the stable-lad!

This man really did deserve the humiliation she hoped he suffered once Stephen told him she was his daughter, rather than his lover, Angelica decided with tight-lipped annoyance.

'After you.' Wolf gave an abrupt inclination of his superior head, his sculptured mouth unsmiling.

Angelica had to nudge the mare twice in the ribs to get her to walk across the cobbles towards the bridle path she usually took when she went riding with Stephen, taking a few minutes to get her bearings in the saddle, not having been down to Stephen's country estate for several weeks now.

There really hadn't been the opportunity for Angelica to take riding lessons when she was younger, and Stephen had decided to rectify that once she'd started staying with him. To her relief, she could now sit in the saddle without fear of falling, although she was a more nervous rider than she would have wished.

She certainly wasn't a match for Wolf Gambrelli's easy, natural seat; rider and horse seemed to move as one, she acknowledged admiringly as he preceded her down the bridle path and out onto the fields beyond. He controlled the grey effortlessly, the muscles rippling in his shoulders and back as he did so, his hair moving silkily in the gentle summer breeze.

It was a pity he was the type of man that he was, Angelica thought as she watched the play of muscles across the broad width of Wolf Gambrelli's back; she hadn't been this physically aware of a man in a long time.

If ever!

She wasn't dating anyone at the moment, but at twenty-six she had obviously had several boyfriends in the past. But that was exactly what they had been—*boy*friends.

She had never met anyone quite like Wolf Gambrelli before—a man who exuded a sensuality that made it impossible not to be completely aware of him at all times.

'Just how experienced are you?'

Her wandering thoughts came to a sudden halt as she looked across at him and saw the barely concealed contempt in his hooded gaze. 'Not very,' she replied.

Let him carry on digging that hole, she told herself determinedly. And she hoped, once he knew the truth, that Wolf Gambrelli would cringe in shame for each of the insults he had deliberately dealt her!

Wolf's mouth twisted derisively. He found Angelica's claim very hard to believe, when she obviously had a man of Stephen's experience so completely captivated.

When, much as he hated to admit it, her every move had *him* captivated too!

He gave a terse inclination of his head. 'Perhaps you would like to show me what you can do?' he invited hardly.

Her mouth tightened. 'Perhaps I would,' she returned tartly.

Wolf watched as she urged her horse into a trot beside his, the warm breeze flattening her shirt against her breasts, their hardened tips showing a deep rose through the silky material—at least answering one of the questions he had about her!

But he had many others…

Why she was wasting her youth and considerable beauty on a man so much older, for one? Had she chosen to take Stephen as her lover because she felt an older man would appreciate her youth and beauty in a way that a younger man didn't? Did she think that a man of some years was more likely to remain enthralled by her love-liness? To remain faithful?

If that was what she believed about Stephen, then she had chosen the wrong man—Stephen hadn't been faithful to the wife he had loved, let alone to any of the numerous mistresses he'd had over the years!

'How did you and Stephen meet?' Wolf asked as their horses trotted side by side, with Angelica showing a natural aptitude that he couldn't help but admire, moving easily with the horse, her hands light on the reins.

She gave him a sideways glance before answering guardedly. 'How did Stephen tell you we'd met?'

Wolf gave an appreciative grin at the way she had sensed his question was a trap. 'He didn't,' he responded. 'Only that he hadn't found you, but that you had been the one to find him.'

She smiled, revealing small pearly-white teeth against her red lipgloss. 'It's true—I did.'

And? Wolf wondered frustratedly.

'You are aware that Stephen does not have a history of—fidelity?' he said aloud.

Her smile faded slightly at the same time as her

chin rose in challenge. 'Any more than you do, Count Gambrelli,' she bit out scathingly.

His mouth tightened at the reference to his own reputation. 'We are not discussing me—'

'Aren't we?' Angelica interrupted. 'Then perhaps we should.' Her eyes flashed deeply grey. 'Because it seems to me that you have absolutely no right to comment on Stephen's lack of fidelity when you are obviously such a womaniser yourself!' Her cheeks were flushed with indignant anger on Stephen's behalf.

How dared Wolf Gambrelli presume to comment on Stephen's behaviour when his own numerous relationships were such public knowledge?

He looked down the haughty length of his nose at her. 'You should not believe everything you read in the gutter press!'

Angelica gave a derisive snort. 'If only half the stories of your affairs are true, then that makes you something of a sexual athlete in my book— Let go of my reins, Count Gambrelli!' she warned him nervously as he reached out and grabbed them, drawing her horse closer to his—something the black mare took exception to, if the way it moved skittishly was any indication. 'You'll pull us both out of the saddle in a minute!' she said impatiently as she struggled to maintain control of her horse.

Despite her inexperience she had never become unseated yet—but there was always a first time!

She was finding Wolf Gambrelli's obsession with her relationship with Stephen deeply irritating. Couldn't he see that it really wasn't any of his business? That it wasn't anyone else's business but her own and Stephen's?

It was because of the delicacy, the newness of their father-daughter relationship, that she and Stephen had decided from the onset that it wasn't yet a subject for public consumption. Stephen was all too aware, after years of having his every move reported in the newspapers, of just how the advent of an illegitimate daughter into his life could be sensationalised in the press.

But Wolf Gambrelli was like a dog—a wolf?—gnawing at a bone, refusing to be dissuaded from discussing a subject that was absolutely none of his business.

'I—said—let—go!' she repeated desperately as her horse continued to shift nervously. At the same time she slapped the end of her reins hard across Wolf Gambrelli's restraining hand, digging her heels into her horse's flanks as she felt Wolf briefly relax his grip at the sting of her strike. Bending low over the mare's mane, Angelica urged her mount into a gallop.

But she could hear Wolf Gambrelli's immediate pursuit of her, the thunder of the grey's hooves close behind her, could almost feel its hot breath against her thighs as it began to gain on her.

She dug her heels even harder into her mare's flanks, not caring at that moment that she had never galloped a horse as fast as this before, that she no longer felt completely in control. She was intent on getting away from Wolf Gambrelli—on getting away from his increasingly insulting remarks.

'Stop, you little fool!' he shouted to her impatiently.

Angelica ignored him, too busy concentrating on maintaining her seat in the saddle to even attempt to answer him. Her eyes widened in panic as she saw the mare wasn't going in the direction of the open gate, but was instead rapidly approaching the four-foot wall that bordered the field. Her own frantic pulling on the reins seemed to have no effect on its nervous flight.

She wasn't sure what happened next—whether the mare had suddenly decided she didn't want to jump the wall after all, or if her own desperate pulling on the reins to get the horse to stop had finally had some effect. All Angelica was aware of was the horse coming to a sudden slithering halt, and her own momentum taking her up and over the mare's head. Briefly she had a feeling as if she were flying, before landing so hard on her back on the ground that all the breath seemed to have been knocked from her body, forcing her to close her eyes as the world began to spin wildly around her.

Wolf had ground his teeth frustratedly as he'd watched Angelica gallop away from him, his eyes widening as he realised she had lost control of her horse. Instantly he had urged the grey in pursuit, and had almost been within touching distance of her reins when the mare had decided to come to an abrupt halt. Wolf's face had paled, and he'd been able to do nothing but watch in horror as Angelica sailed over the mare's head, to land on her back with a sickening thump several feet away on the hard ground.

Now, he pulled on the grey's reins, barely waiting for the horse to come to a stop before sliding quickly out of his saddle and running over to where Angelica still lay stunned—dead?—on the ground.

'You little fool!' he ground out harshly, even as he went down on his knees beside her.

He didn't feel in the least reassured by her closed, unmoving lids and the pallor of her cheeks, and pulled her roughly against him. Her hair, loosened from its band, cascaded silkily over his arm.

'Why did you not listen to me?' he rasped fiercely. 'Angel…? *Angel!*' he urged more forcefully as he saw a pulse beating reassuringly at the delicacy of her temple. 'For God's sake, open your eyes and look at me!' he muttered harshly, relieved beyond belief to find she was still alive, but now needing to know whether or not she had broken any bones in the fall.

Her eyes remained firmly closed, but her throat moved convulsively and she spoke. 'If you don't mind, I'd really rather not,' she murmured.

Wolf sighed his frustration with her comment. 'Rather not *what?*' he demanded impatiently.

Was she delirious? Had the fall somehow muddled her brain? What—?

'Look at you,' she answered him wryly. 'This is embarrassing enough as it is, without that!'

'Embarrassing…?' he repeated uncertainly as his arms tightened their hold about her. 'Angel, if you don't open your eyes now and assure me that you haven't broken anything, then I am going to be forced into giving you a sound shaking!' he warned.

Angelica raised her lids with effort, relieved that the world seemed to have stopped spinning at least, a rueful smile curving her lips as she looked up into Wolf Gambrelli's angry face. 'And that's really going to help!' she commented wryly, not sure that she *hadn't* broken anything, most of her still feeling numb from her sudden impact with the ground.

No, it didn't feel as if anything were broken, she decided as she slowly flexed the muscles in her arms and legs. Her back was feeling bruised, but not particularly painful. Her teeth had been soundly rattled, but as she ran her tongue over them she could feel that they were all still in place too.

She looked up to find Wolf looking anxiously down at her. Their gazes locked, and Angelica watched in fascination as the pupils in those dark brown eyes became so enlarged that there seemed to be no brown left, only black. His dark gaze shifted down suddenly, to the parted softness of her mouth.

Wolf Gambrelli was going to kiss her...!

Angelica became absolutely sure of that fact only a second before his head lowered and his mouth claimed hers in fierce demand, his arms like steel bands about her as he held her close against the hardness of his chest.

She was too disorientated, too shaken up to do anything other than respond to the hard demand of Wolf's lips on hers. The angry assault on her mouth came too quickly after her fall. Her arms moved up to cling to his shoulders and she once again felt as if she were flying through the air without the benefit of a safety net.

His hair felt just as soft and silky as she had imagined it would as she moved her hand and her fingers became entangled in its thickness. Her other hand was still clinging to the broadness of his shoulder, feeling the tension of the muscles as Wolf strained her ever closer to him, his lips moving against hers with a thoroughness that completely robbed her of resistance.

Her lips parted as she felt the demanding rasp of his tongue against their softness, and he explored their sensitivity before seeking further, that tongue becoming a hard thrust as he laid her down on the ground and came down beside her, his hands moving restlessly over her body from breast to thigh and then back again, impatiently pushing the soft material of her shirt aside to cup her nakedness.

It was too much after the mare's recent flight and her absolute panic as she saw the wall approaching; Angelica had absolutely no will to fight this almost angry onslaught.

Instead she groaned at the sweet pleasure that suddenly coursed through her body, at the increasing warmth between her thighs, her breasts tingling achingly as Wolf moved his mouth from hers to trail heated kisses down her jaw and throat.

The heat of his lips and mouth captured one turgid nipple, and his tongue began to lave moistly across that sensitive peak before suckling her fully into the hot cavern beyond.

Angelica's back arched in pleasure as Wolf's hand captured and caressed her other breast. The heat between her thighs was increasing to a dangerous level, becoming a deep, aching need as Wolf sucked harder on her breast, at the same time moving his tongue moistly against her. But that mouth was suddenly wrenched away, and Wolf looked down at her disbelievingly. 'No!' he groaned protestingly, even as he put her roughly away from him to stand up, his hands clenched tightly at his sides as he stared down at her. 'You belong to another man!'

Angelica tried to focus, totally disorientated from her fall, let alone Wolf's assault on her senses.

Wolf closed his eyes, then opened them as he said, 'It is against my honour—against every rule that I— For God's sake cover yourself!' he instructed harshly, his face deathly pale beneath his natural tan, a nerve pulsing in his tightly clenched jaw.

Wolf's self-loathing, the contempt in his voice for her, lashed at Angelica as she pulled her shirt back together and scrambled to her feet. Turning her back on him, she moved stiffly to check on her horse as it cropped the grass a few feet away, her knees trembling, her hands shaking slightly as she touched the warmth of the mare's still quivering neck.

What a stupid, *stupid* thing for her to have done!

Not that she'd had any choice in the matter— she'd been too stunned after her fall to resist when Wolf began to kiss her with such urgent demand. But to have allowed herself to respond to Wolf's kisses and caresses—to groan that response out loud!—had been the height of stupidity on her part.

Because she didn't *want* to respond to this man Wolf Gambrelli, who was just a younger version of Stephen—a man who only stayed around long enough to break a woman's heart before moving on to his next conquest.

And to respond to Wolf Gambrelli had been especially stupid—had only served to increase his contempt for her. Now Wolf didn't only believe her to be the lover of a man thirty years older than she was, but he also thought she was the *unfaithful* lover of a man thirty years her senior!

Well, it was time—past time!—that someone set him straight on both those points!

'Wolf, I think you should know that Stephen is—'

'A fool,' he grated disgustedly. 'As am I, for also succumbing to your tricks!'

Angelica stared at him incredulously. 'You think I *deliberately* got myself thrown from my horse? That I actually engineered what happened just now?'

Wolf looked at her coldly, still inwardly battling against the arousal that had claimed him so completely when he'd held Angelica in his arms. His relief that she wasn't dead after all had been followed by anger at her stupidity in racing off in that reckless way, compelling him into kissing and caressing her in that wild, abandoned way.

It didn't help that he was also inwardly battling with the fact that he had broken his own cardinal rule of never poaching on another man's prior claim to a woman!

His mouth thinned. 'I did not say that—'

'You didn't need to put it into actual words.' Angelica breathed angrily, her breasts—the nipples still hard and aroused from his caresses!—quickly rising and falling beneath her shirt. 'You are incredible, Wolf—do you know that?' she continued heatedly. 'You took advantage of the fact that I was stunned, if not totally disorientated, after being thrown from my horse, and now you're turning the whole incident back on *me*!' She shook her head. 'My God, you deserve the humiliation that is most assuredly coming your way! The sooner the better, as far as I'm concerned!'

Wolf became very still, his gaze narrowing on her angrily flushed face. 'What do you mean?' he finally asked.

'Oh, no, Count Gambrelli,' Angelica scorned. 'After the things you've said—done—I'm not going to make it that easy for you! Suffice to say that when you finally know the truth I look forward to seeing you on your knees in abject apology!' she told him angrily.

'You will wait a long time!' Wolf assured her.

She shook her head, the smile she gave him completely humourless. 'I have a feeling you may be wrong about that!'

Wolf didn't take to the confidence in her tone at all. What truth was she talking about? And did it have anything to do with Stephen's ulterior motive in inviting him here this weekend?

Her mouth turned down with obvious contempt. 'I'm going back to the house now,' she said tautly, leading the mare over to the gate and using that as leverage for swinging herself back up into the saddle. 'I would appreciate it if you stayed well away from me for the remainder of your stay!' she added, her eyes flashing deeply grey as she looked down at him.

She need have no worries there—after what had happened, Wolf had no intention of spending any more time alone in her company than he absolutely had to!

In fact, he had no intention of remaining here longer than he had to!

Wolf stared after her as she turned the horse and cantered away, his gaze narrowed speculatively.

Angelica was staying here with Stephen. She had visited the other man's bedroom late at night. Stephen obviously adored her, even if her own emotions were harder to clarify.

What truth was Angelica talking about that could possibly make those things other than what they were?

CHAPTER FOUR

'WHAT would you like to do after lunch?'

Angelica was already struggling to eat the delicious roast chicken that had been prepared for Sunday lunch. Stephen's lightly spoken query killed her appetite completely. Because she didn't want to do anything that might involve Wolf Gambrelli.

Arrogant, hypocritical bastard that he was!

She had soaked in the bath for an hour once she'd returned to the house earlier this morning, hoping to avoid the pain and stiffness that were sure to result from her tumble. She had succeeded for the main part, although her back still ached a little.

But there had been no way she could avoid sitting down to lunch without alerting Stephen to the fact that something was wrong. And she would rather he didn't worry himself about her self-inflicted fall.

The fact that she and Wolf had only addressed

remarks to Stephen during the meal, and never to each other, should have alerted Stephen to the fact that something was definitely going on between the two of them. Except he was obviously distracted himself...

'Unfortunately I have to return to London after lunch.' Wolf was the one to answer distantly. 'My cousin called me a short time ago to tell me that his wife gave birth to a daughter early this morning. I would like to visit them later today.'

Angelica was so startled by the vision his words painted that she could only stare at him in surprise. Wolf Gambrelli didn't give the impression that he was particularly interested in babies—newborn or otherwise!

His mouth quirked as he obviously saw her reaction. 'You did not think that I had a family?' he prompted coolly.

'I can't say I had given the subject any thought,' Angelica came back with tart honesty.

Wolf raised blond brows cryptically. 'Besides my cousin, I have a mother still living, and a younger brother, Luc.'

'How nice,' Angelica said insincerely, receiving a sceptical look for her trouble.

Well, she wasn't interested in Wolf Gambrelli's family. Wasn't interested in *him*. Was she...?

'Cesare has a daughter?' Stephen spoke to the other man warmly. 'I hope he's prepared to have his heart broken!' he teased.

Wolf gave the older man a quizzical glance. 'But I understand that both Robin and the baby are well…'

'It's in about twenty years—well, maybe twenty-five—that he'll have his heart broken!' Stephen assured Wolf dryly. 'When some other man comes along and steals her away from him. Believe me, no-one will be good enough!'

Angelica got up from the table. 'I'll see about having coffee served on the terrace.'

Stephen reached out to grasp her hand as she passed by him. 'You seem a little tense, darling. Is everything all right?'

Wolf looked at Angelica, noting the slight pallor to her cheeks. Perhaps she had hurt herself this morning, after all…?

'Angelica took a fall from her horse this morning—'

'Why didn't you tell me, Angel?' Stephen cut in sharply, standing up. 'Are you hurt? What the hell happened?'

Angelica shot Wolf a reproving look before answering Stephen reassuringly. 'Nothing happened,' she said brightly. 'I just fell off, that's all. I'm completely okay. No bones broken.' She smiled reassuringly.

'Perhaps I should take you to A&E at the local hospital and have them check you out anyway,' Stephen declared, still looking at Angelica searchingly. 'If anything should happen to you—'

'It won't,' she assured him. 'And I don't need a doctor. It was only my pride that was hurt,' she added ruefully.

Wolf felt as if a knife had sliced through him at the concern he could hear in Angelica's voice as she reassured Stephen of her welfare, and realised that she did care for the other man, after all...

He had tried not to think about what had happened between the two of them this morning—had told himself it was a momentary madness. That once he was safely back in London he would be able to put the fickle Angelica Harper from his mind.

But as he heard that concern—love?—in her voice for Stephen, he knew that he was only fooling himself, that whether he liked it or not, Angelica Harper had got under his skin!

And he didn't like it. Didn't want to be attracted to a woman who so obviously belonged to another man.

'Please reassure him, Wolf.' She turned to enlist

his help. 'Tell him I was on my feet and back up in the saddle almost immediately.'

Almost immediately…

It was what had happened during that period of 'almost immediately' that had precipitated Wolf's decision to return to London earlier than planned.

Oh, Cesare *had* telephoned him earlier this morning to tell him of his daughter's birth, and Wolf *did* intend visiting mother and baby this evening. But it was his need to get away, as far away from Angelica Harper as possible, that had made him decide to leave earlier than he had intended.

His manner was deliberately enigmatic as he looked at Stephen. 'I can assure you that Angelica was not in the least hurt by the fall,' he said.

Implying what? Angelica wondered, very aware of how ambiguous Wolf's words had been. Surely he didn't think he had hurt her earlier with his accusations? It would take a lot more than Wolf Gambrelli's mistaken assumptions about her to do that!

'There—you see,' she told Stephen brightly. 'I'm fine. Really,' He didn't look convinced, so she encouraged, 'Now, let's go out onto the terrace for coffee. Wolf has to leave shortly,' she finished pointedly.

'I really wish you had told me about your

accident, Angel.' Stephen was still looking anxious as he accompanied her outside onto the terrace.

'I told you—it was nothing,' she dismissed with a husky laugh. 'And my tumble certainly wasn't graceful!'

'I don't believe you could ever do anything that wasn't graceful,' Stephen chided affectionately, and he linked his fingers with hers.

Wolf, following behind them, saw the intimacy of that gesture, and his mouth tightened with displeasure. He really couldn't stand to watch the emotional bond between these two much longer!

'I think perhaps I will forgo the coffee,' he said stiffly. 'I need to pack my things—'

'I'm sure you have time to sit and drink a cup of coffee with us, Wolf.' Stephen turned to him, a smile on his face. 'Charming as Cesare's daughter no doubt is, she isn't going to notice if her second cousin arrives a little later than planned! Besides,' he added frowningly, 'and I know I've been putting this off.' His expression became a grimace. 'But I really do have something I need to discuss with you before you go.'

Wolf's gaze narrowed on Angelica, but her eyes met his unflinchingly.

Was his discussion with Stephen to include a

reference to his passionate moment with Angelica earlier today?

Stephen's manner hadn't been angry or aggressive during lunch, though, which meant the other man was probably referring to his mysterious ulterior motive for inviting Wolf here this weekend.

Whatever, the sooner this discussion was over the better; Wolf certainly didn't intend staying on here for the rest of the day and behaving like a complete hypocrite.

He had overstepped a line with Angelica Harper this morning, and at the same time had betrayed his friendship with Stephen. The wisest thing to do was remove himself from further temptation.

'This isn't to be a business discussion, is it?' Angelica asked Stephen. 'Because you promised me that you only had that conference call to deal with this weekend,' she reminded him, as she sat down at the table to pour out three cups of coffee.

Stephen grinned across at Wolf where he lounged in one of the wicker chairs. 'It's so nice to have someone fussing over me again,' he admitted. 'You really should try it some time!' he pronounced warmly as Angelica handed him a cup of the coffee she had just poured.

Considering Wolf had spent the best part of his

thirty-six years avoiding such an occurrence, he couldn't see that changing in the next decade!

'Count Gambrelli…?' Angelica gave him his coffee, deliberately not looking at Wolf and avoiding her hand coming into contact with his.

Those long hands, sensitive hands, that had caressed her so intimately earlier…

She winced with embarrassment every time she thought of that time in Wolf's arms. A man whose way of life was complete anathema to her. Because he was a man who took what he wanted and to hell with the consequences.

A man exactly like Stephen. And *she* had been the consequence…

Admittedly Wolf wasn't married, but Angelica certainly wasn't about to fall into the same trap that her mother had and make the mistake of being attracted to a man whose affairs were legendary!

'Is this the same something you mentioned briefly last night, Stephen, or something else?' Wolf Gambrelli asked conversationally.

At least it sounded like a casual query, but nevertheless Angelica could hear the steely edge to his voice—as if he suspected this wasn't going to be a pleasant chat at all.

Surely he didn't think she had told Stephen what had happened between the two of them earlier?

She really wasn't that stupid. Knowing Stephen as she now did, and knowing how mischievous his sense of humour could be, he would probably find it highly amusing that she had actually allowed a man so like himself to get past her guard. Stephen was totally aware of the fact that Angelica disapproved of the way he had behaved during his marriage; honesty had been a prerequisite to them finding some sort of relationship together.

Stephen's smile faded as he turned to the younger man. 'I've been putting off discussing this with you all week, but—Wolf, on Tuesday morning I'm booking into a private clinic. I would like to say it's nothing serious.' He paused, seeming sad. 'But that would only be kidding myself. After years of believing I didn't even have one, my heart has decided to make its presence felt, and I have to have an operation to correct a problem.'

Angelica swallowed hard, her eyes misting over with tears at Stephen's easy explanation of the seriousness of the operation he was about to have.

She had deemed it ironic—tragic, even—that only months after she had made contact with Stephen his heart problem had been discovered. But Stephen had refused to deal with the gravity of his condition, using getting to know her as an excuse to put off treatment, and only consenting to the operation now because he had absolutely no choice: he either had surgery, or he would shortly die.

Although quite what that had to do with Wolf Gambrelli, Angel had no idea...

Of course the two men were involved in several business deals together, so perhaps Stephen felt he owed it to the younger man to tell him how ill he was?

She turned slightly as she sensed Wolf's eyes on her, her expression becoming deliberately bland as she saw the censure in his face. No doubt he believed her, as Stephen's young and beautiful new mistress, to be partly to blame for the strain on Stephen's heart!

Wolf's mouth thinned as he looked at Angelica. She exhibited none of his own surprise at Stephen's illness, so obviously she already knew about it. That knowledge brought to the fore numerous questions Wolf would rather not know the answers to!

He turned back to the older man. 'And the prognosis?' he prompted with his usual directness.

'Fifty-fifty,' Stephen acknowledged heavily. 'But if I don't have the op it's a hundred per cent certain I'm going to die in the next six months,' he revealed brutally.

'Stephen...!' Angelica groaned.

'Now, we've discussed this, Angel.' Stephen sat forward to grasp her hand in one of his. 'I'm not scared of dying. In fact, if it weren't for you, I don't think I would bother with this operation at all. Having you in my life this last year, wanting you to stay in my life for a lot longer, has been what's finally decided me to go through with this operation.' He smiled encouragingly.

Wolf shifted uncomfortably. The affection between these two was more apparent than ever. He felt even more guilty about his behaviour with Angelica this morning now that he knew how ill Stephen was…

'What would you like me to do?' he asked Stephen briskly.

The older man gave him an appreciative smile. 'I knew you would understand, Wolf. The thing is, I'm worried about Angel if anything should happen to me—'

'I'm sure I'm not going to need Count Gambrelli's help in the unlikely event of that happening!' Angelica gasped protestingly.

'That's just the problem, Angel. You are,' Stephen insisted. 'My business life is a tangled web that only another businessman could possibly understand. Besides which, half my business dealings are linked to Wolf's anyway.'

Wolf could clearly see Angelica's dismay at the thought of his involvement if the worst should happen to Stephen. Because Wolf could now clearly see through her involvement with the older man? Or because she had responded to his kisses this morning…?

Stephen sighed again. 'I did warn you I had invited you here this weekend with an ulterior motive, Wolf. I wanted you to meet Angel—get to know her. We've been friends for years, you're the closest thing I have to a son, and—with your agreement—I would like to make you joint executor of my will with my lawyer. Angel doesn't need to be bothered with things like that if I should die. Besides, being the sole heir pretty much excludes her from becoming an executor—'

'Please stop, Stephen!' Angelica pleaded emotionally. 'I told you from the beginning that I don't want anything from you—'

'I don't have anyone else to leave it to, darling,' he reasoned gently.

'That isn't the point,' Angelica responded, deliberately not looking at Wolf Gambrelli, even though she had sensed his piercingly scathing glance on her since Stephen had revealed she was to be his sole heir.

No doubt this knowledge fitted in perfectly with

Wolf's opinion of her using an older man's infatuation for her to get her hands on his money!

'You are *not* going to die,' she told Stephen fiercely. 'I simply won't let you!'

He laughed indulgently. 'I wish it were that easy, darling. But we both know it's not. And I want to make provision for you after I'm gone. Wolf is the perfect man to deal with all this. I know it's a lot to ask, Wolf, but would you do this for me?' He looked expectantly at the younger man.

Angelica looked at Wolf Gambrelli too, her expression deliberately challenging as she met his stare. For once his thoughts weren't hidden behind that lazily arrogant façade. His derision towards her was clearly there for her to see, before he masked his feelings and turned back to Stephen.

'Let us hope that will not be necessary—'

'All the hoping in the world isn't going to make it fact,' Stephen cut in practically. 'Besides, even if the operation is a success, Angel is still going to need a strong shoulder to lean on for some weeks—'

'But not Wolf's!' Angelica found herself protesting fiercely, delicate colour warming her cheeks as she realised just how vehement she sounded. 'We don't even *know* each other,' she attempted to argue, deliberately not meeting Wolf's eyes as she sensed him watching her from beneath lowered lids.

Stephen's expression softened. 'Darling, that's the whole reason for bringing the two of you together this weekend.'

So *this* was why Stephen had seemed to thrust the two of them together this weekend, Wolf realised. He was deeply concerned by the seriousness of Stephen's illness—but even more disturbed at the idea of being that strong shoulder for Angelica to lean on following Stephen's operation, or worse!

Wolf had already betrayed his friend once this morning, and the thought of days, possibly weeks, of being at Angel's side while Stephen recovered—*if* he recovered!—from his operation, was impossible for Wolf to even contemplate.

As it obviously was for Angelica!

But how could Wolf say no to Stephen's heartfelt request? As far as he knew Stephen had no family of his own, and the two of them had been friends and business associates for a long time. In the circumstances, Wolf knew he had to be Stephen's first choice as executor and as a protector for Stephen's Angel…!

'You should have shared your illness with me earlier, Stephen.'

The older man shrugged. 'No one likes to admit they're getting old,' he replied.

Especially if you had taken a mistress thirty years younger than yourself!

Was this the truth Angelica had been referring to this morning? Did she really think that Stephen's illness made any difference to Wolf's opinion of her? If anything, it did the opposite!

'Besides,' Stephen continued, 'I didn't want to alarm my stockholders. With you at the helm while I'm—incapacitated, that isn't going to happen.'

That was logical—more than logical—and Wolf was more than happy to help Stephen in that way.

It was still being that 'strong shoulder to lean on' for Angelica that posed the real problem for him!

For one thing, it wasn't his shoulder that he wanted the beautiful Angelica to lean on. And the events of this morning could not happen again when she so obviously belonged to another man—a man, moreover, who was a friend and seriously ill! For another, she looked no more happy at the arrangement than Wolf did himself…

Angelica listened to the exchange with growing apprehension. Now she knew the reason Stephen had invited Wolf here for the weekend.

Oh, everything Stephen said made logical sense. Wolf Gambrelli's own success in the board-room made him the perfect person to caretake Stephen's own business interests while he was unable to do it himself. Even asking the other man to be executor of his will, should the worst happen, was a logical choice.

It was the thought of him being such a presence in her own life that was so impossible!

Why was it?

Because he had kissed and caressed her? Or was it because of the way she had responded?

Her honesty, even with herself, insisted that she admit it was the latter…!

She had never responded to any man in the way she had to Wolf Gambrelli this morning. Never experienced that complete melting of her resistance, her body burning with a need that she had known Wolf could more than satisfy.

The very last man she should ever be attracted to!

'Stephen,' she began tentatively, 'I really think this is asking too much of Count Gambrelli.'

Stephen looked at the younger man. 'Is it, Wolf?'

Wolf stood up to walk over to the ornate balustrade that edged the terrace, staring sightlessly out across the manicured lawns and multicoloured flowerbeds, his expression grim as he reached out to tightly grasp the top of that balustrade, his knuckles showing white.

Attracted to Angelica as he was, this was an impossible situation for him to find himself in. But, at the same time, Wolf knew there was no way he could refuse Stephen's request—that his years of friendship with the older man precluded him giving Stephen anything other than an affirmative answer.

Wolf knew himself to be a man always in command of his emotions. Including desire. Surely, for the sake of his friendship with Stephen, he could control this burning need that he had to know Angelica intimately and everything else be damned?

He drew in a ragged breath, his jaw clenching. It was not going to be easy, but honour demanded that he do this for Stephen.

'I'm sorry. This has been—something of a shock,' Wolf told his friend slowly as he turned. 'Of course I will do anything that I can to help,' he assured him, as he strolled back to resume his seat, deliberately not looking at Angelica as he sensed her dismay at his answer.

'Thank you, Wolf. I knew I could count on your support.' Stephen reached out and shook him warmly by the hand.

Wolf nodded in stiff acknowledgement. 'I will do everything I can to be of assistance to Angelica during this difficult time.'

'You don't know what a relief that is,' Stephen said. 'The last thing Angel is going to need is the press hearing of my stay in the clinic, noticing

Angel's visits, and sniffing around to add two and two together and coming up with the right answer of four!'

Wolf's expression sharpened. 'Two and two...?'

'Stephen—'

'Angel, Wolf can't protect you if he doesn't know what he's protecting you from.'

'I don't need protecting,' she protested agitatedly.

'I disagree,' Stephen insisted gently. 'We've deliberately kept our relationship strictly between ourselves, Wolf,' he said ruefully as he turned to the younger man, 'but I think you need to know the truth—'

'Stephen—'

'If Wolf is to be of any help to you at all then he has to know the truth, Angel,' Stephen insisted firmly. 'Wolf—this beautiful creature, this wonderful woman—my lovely, lovely Angel—is the daughter I never dreamed I would have!' he announced emotionally.

Stephen's daughter! Wolf echoed hollowly to himself, even as he masked the deep shock he felt at the revelation.

Angel was Stephen's *daughter?*

'We've kept the whole thing private because we wanted to avoid any speculation or gossip.' Stephen reached out to squeeze Angel's hand.

'But you need to know the truth, Wolf, if you're to protect Angel from any unwanted publicity.'

Wolf quickly thought back over the last twenty hours or so, since he had first been introduced to Angelica, remembering Stephen's pride in her, his obvious love for her. Feelings that Wolf had assumed to be those of a besotted lover.

But which could equally be the pride and love of a father!

A father, if Wolf guessed correctly, who hadn't even known of his daughter's existence until a year ago!

This was the truth that Angelica had warned Wolf would bring him to his knees in abject apology.

The only person Wolf felt like bringing to her knees was Angelica herself—as he administered the sound telling-off she so richly deserved for continuing to deceive him in the way she had!

CHAPTER FIVE

'COME to apologise, Count Gambrelli?' Angelica challenged, as she opened her bedroom door to find him standing outside in the hallway.

She had excused herself a short time ago, leaving Wolf and Stephen on the terrace to discuss the business side of their arrangement, knowing her presence wasn't necessary for that, and needing some time alone to think over the fact that Wolf Gambrelli was probably going to be a permanent fixture in her life for the next week at the very least.

He had hidden his reaction well earlier when Stephen had revealed that she was his daughter. Only the tight clenching of his jaw and the steely-eyed glare he had given her had revealed the deep shock that he'd felt. A steely-eyed glare that, unless she was mistaken, had promised retribution rather than apology!

'I hardly think so,' he said now, and he eased

past her into the bedroom to close the door firmly behind him, then lean back against it and survey her.

'I don't remember inviting you into my bedroom, Count Gambrelli.' Angelica continued to face him defiantly. Only the rapid beat of her heart and the slight trembling of the hands she put behind her back revealed that she wasn't as confident as she wanted to appear.

His mouth twisted. 'You knew when you excused yourself earlier that I would come up to your bedroom at the first opportunity,' he responded hardly. 'In fact, you probably counted on my doing exactly that!'

Her eyes widened at the accusation. 'No—'

'Yes!' Wolf rasped forcefully, his anger barely under control as he breathed raggedly, his hands in fists clenched at his sides. 'Tell me, Angel, have you enjoyed the little game you have been playing with me?'

'I wasn't playing with you at all,' she protested, taking a step back from his barely controlled anger. 'And only Stephen calls me—'

'Angel?' Wolf questioned hardly, taking that same step forward. 'But you are no angel, are you?' he commented as his gaze swept over her contemptuously, lingering on the rapid rise and fall of the creamy swell of her breasts. 'You were aware that I desired you from the moment we first met.'

'No—'

'Oh, yes, Angel,' he breathed with deliberation. 'And you have enjoyed watching me battle between that desire and the friendship I have with Stephen— which prevented me doing anything about it!'

The anger he felt towards this woman had been steadily boiling during the last half an hour, increasing in temperature—though none of that inner turmoil had been apparent when he'd discussed business with Stephen downstairs on the terrace. The other man had seemed completely unaware of Wolf's reaction to learning that Angel was his daughter rather than his lover, as Wolf had assumed her to be.

But his anger had now reached explosion point!

'It was a completely unnecessary battle, as it turns out,' Wolf continued softly, even as he reached out to clasp her arms and pull her up against him. He crushed her breasts against his chest, their creaminess no longer a temptation he intended to deny himself.

'Stop this *now*!' Angelica advised breathlessly, as she felt the effect of the warmth of Wolf's body pressed against her own, his legs, taut and muscled as he drew her more intimately against him, making her completely aware of the hardness of his arousal. 'Wolf, Stephen and I agreed from the beginning that we wouldn't tell anyone of our relationship, that we had to get to know each other first—it wasn't only my secret to tell!' she protested.

Then she saw the intent in Wolf's eyes as he began to lower his mouth to hers, taking possession of her mouth in a kiss that was designed to punish, to convey his deep anger. And in that it succeeded.

But, after her initial resistance, it also aroused in Angelica a fierce desire that more than equalled Wolf's...

They kissed hungrily, taking from each other, and Wolf's arms were like steel bands about her body as he moulded her against him. Her own arms moved up about his shoulders and her hands became entangled in the silky thickness of his thick blond hair, encouraging his plundering mouth to deeper intimacies—an invitation Wolf took complete advantage of, as his tongue plunged searchingly into the cavern of her mouth, seeking, learning, knowing her with an intimacy that made Angelica groan achingly. Eventually she opened dazed and unfocused eyes to look up at him as he wrenched his mouth from hers.

'Not here, Angel,' Wolf grated as brought her arms firmly down to her sides. 'And certainly not now. When I make love to you it will be at a time and place of my own choosing.'

'*When?*' Angelica repeated, her heart still beating rapidly, her breasts still aching with the need to feel his touch again. 'Aren't you being a little arrogant in assuming there will ever be a *when*?' Her chin rose and her cheeks flamed with embarrassed colour at her inability to even attempt to hide her response to this man.

A response she didn't seem to have any control over…

She had believed her reaction to Wolf this morning had been because she had been slightly dazed and shaken from her fall—had been convinced that she wouldn't have been as acquiescent if she had been in full control of her faculties.

Their hunger for each other just now made a complete mockery of that assumption!

'Am I?' Wolf looked down at her with lazily mocking eyes. 'You do not like it when I do this?' His head lowered as he ran the tip of his tongue along the sensitive line of her lips. 'You like it even less when I do this?' The warmth of his breath moved sensuously against the moisture of her mouth and his hand cupped one of her breasts, the soft pad of his thumb easily finding and caressing its hardened tip.

Angelica arched weakly against him as the warmth spread down her body to her thighs, that rush of heat making her moist and aching as she quivered in response.

Wolf looked down at her, satisfaction gleaming in the depths of his dark eyes. 'Yes, I can see how much you dislike my touch,' he murmured derisively. 'You dislike it so much that you are aching for me to repeat it!'

He was enjoying this, Angelica recognised frustratedly. Was enjoying every moment of humiliating her!

'You're deluding yourself, Count Gambrelli!' she told him heatedly, and she stepped away to glare at him.

'Am I?' Wolf taunted, not in the least convinced by Angel's protests when he could still feel her, taste her, on his senses.

'You most certainly are!' she assured him firmly. 'You are everything that I despise in a man!'

His gaze narrowed dangerously. 'Am I?' he repeated softly.

'Yes!' she repeated fiercely. 'You're a womaniser, a love-them-and-leave-them playboy! A man—'

'Exactly like your real father,' Wolf put in hardly, not in the least amused to hear himself described as such.

Even if it was true…

'Exactly!' she echoed forcefully. 'I've grown to care about Stephen in spite of his faults, to love him because he is my father. But you—a man with the same cavalier attitude to women—you, I don't even have to like!'

Wolf studied her. It was true that he had enjoyed women, lots of women, but they had enjoyed him in return. He had never deliberately meant to hurt any of them by misleading them about the nature of a relationship with him. He had always kept his emotions firmly in control…

He shrugged. 'I believe I could be content with the same lack of liking for me that you displayed a few minutes ago!' he drawled.

'Well, I couldn't,' Angelica came swiftly back. 'I would have to at least respect the man I—I—' She broke off. 'I can assure you I have no intention of becoming the most recent in the long list of your conquests!'

'What a pity for you, then, that I have just assured Stephen that I will care for you in his absence!' Wolf replied levelly, though obviously stung by her scorn.

Angelica could guess just *how* he intended caring for her!

'Doesn't this friendship you claim to feel for Stephen—'

'It is not a claim!' he rejoined intensely. 'Our friendship goes back many years.'

Her brows rose. 'In that case, doesn't this friendship include treating Stephen's daughter with a little respect?' she challenged.

'Perhaps.' Wolf gave an arrogant inclination of his head. 'If,' he continued, 'I were sure of your motives for claiming to be his daughter.'

'I don't claim anything. It's a fact!' she came back tartly.

Those dark eyes glittered. 'And how long have you known this "fact"?'

Angelica's eyes narrowed warily. 'Since I was twelve years old and asked my mother about him.'

Wolf gave a humourless smile. 'And yet you waited until a year ago before contacting him?'

Her cheeks warmed at his implication. 'Because until that time he had a wife who could have been hurt by my mere existence!' she defended indignantly.

'Grace.' He nodded. 'Tell me, Angel, were you prompted to contact Stephen after her death simply out of a sense of curiosity, or was it the fact that he had no rightful heir and the size of his bank balance that interested you?'

Angelica drew in a sharp, painful breath.

It was just these sort of accusations that had

caused her to pause before contacting Stephen a year ago, knowing that certain people would undoubtedly see her behaviour in this light. After the insults Wolf had hurled at her when he had only thought her to be Stephen's mistress, she should have known that he would be one of those people…

She gave him a pitying look. 'Stephen has already told you that I have refused to take anything from him—'

'He's also informed me that you are to be the sole heir in his will,' Wolf reminded her.

Her eyes flashed deeply grey. 'I knew nothing about that until a few minutes ago!'

His mouth quirked. 'But surely you must have guessed?' he pressed. 'Once Grace had died, Stephen had no family other than a long, lost-daughter who suddenly appeared on his doorstep a year ago!'

Angelica could barely speak. 'I think you had better leave my bedroom now, Count Gambrelli,' she instructed coldly. 'Before you say anything more insulting than you already have!'

He eyed her superciliously. 'What is so insulting about pointing out that you will become a very wealthy woman on Stephen's death? Whether that should be in the near future or in several years' time…'

'Will you get out?' she bit out shakily, not even wanting to face the possibility that Stephen might die. 'I'll explain to Stephen, tell him that it's impossible for the two of us to be together—'

'You will explain no such thing!' Wolf corrected her harshly. 'If I have understood this situation correctly, then Stephen is a very sick man…?'

'Yes,' she confirmed huskily.

Wolf nodded abruptly. 'Then he does not need the added worry of his concern for your welfare,' he stated. 'If he should ask, we will assure him that the arrangement he has suggested is completely agreeable to both of us.'

Angelica wanted to disagree with him, but at the same time knew that she couldn't do that. Stephen really didn't need anything more to worry about at the moment other than his own health.

'Don't look so discouraged, Angel,' Wolf drawled. 'The fact that you consider me a libertine and a womaniser, and I suspect you to be nothing more than a beautiful gold-digger, should make for a very interesting few days, don't you think?'

No, she didn't think so at all!

Stephen, out of concern for her, had put her in an untenable position. Something neither she or Wolf could dispute with him at the moment…

Wolf watched the emotions moving rapidly

across Angel's face. Her obvious dismay at the thought of spending any length of time in his company quickly followed by resolve and acceptance of that situation, if only for Stephen's sake.

After years of being pursued by some of the most beautiful women in the world, of having any of those women he'd decided he wanted, perversely Wolf found Angel's obvious reluctance to spend any time with him deeply arousing.

He smiled derisively. 'Stephen and I have discussed the living arrangements for the next week—'

'Living arrangements?' Angel echoed suspiciously. 'What living arrangements?'

Wolf's smile widened. 'I believe you are to stay at Stephen's town house for the next week at least…?'

'It's much closer to the clinic than my apartment,' she confirmed warily.

Wolf gave a mocking inclination of his head. 'Stephen and I have agreed that it would probably be best if I were to stay there too—rather than in my suite at the Gambrelli Hotel on the other side of the city.'

'This is getting ridiculous,' Angel exclaimed. 'I'm twenty-six years old, and certainly not in need of a babysitter!'

Wolf's smile became as wolfish as his name as he enjoyed her discomfort at the thought of sharing a house with him. 'But I don't have the least intention of treating you like a child, Angel,' he assured her.

'I told you not to call me that!' she bit out with an impatient gesture of her hands.

Wolf's gaze roamed in a leisurely fashion over the flushed beauty of her face, searching for some resemblance to Stephen now that he knew the other man was her father.

Stephen's hair had once been as dark as Angel's, but his eyes were blue rather than that smoky grey, and Angel's features were much finer, her face heart-shaped. There was perhaps a similarity in the shape of her brows and the determined tilt of her chin…

'I admit, you are more of a dark angel than the golden kind,' Wolf drawled appreciatively. 'But I think I would prefer my Angel to be a little— wicked rather than angelic!'

'I am not your Angel and I never will be!' Angelica glared at him frustratedly. 'If we really are to share a house for the next week, Count Gambrelli—'

'Oh we are,' he confirmed softly.

Her mouth firmed. 'In that case, I would appreciate it if during that time you would refrain from making any personal remarks of a questionable nature. In fact—' She broke off as Wolf laughed to himself. 'I don't see anything in the least funny about this situation!' she told him with another glare.

He shrugged. 'That is because, for the moment, you seem to have lost your sense of humour,' he observed.

'And you seem to have finally found yours!' she accused, disgruntled.

She didn't believe she had ever found her own sense of humour around this man! He annoyed her, irritated her…and aroused her. But she certainly hadn't found anything about him in the least amusing.

Especially her own response to him…

Wolf had been rude to her from the beginning, suspicious of her motives—and he seemed to be even more suspicious now that he knew she was Stephen's long-lost daughter.

There was no way she should have physically responded to this man!

And yet she had…

Her chin rose determinedly. '*If* we're to share a house—'

'I have told you that we are,' Wolf confirmed.

She nodded. 'Then, Count Gambrelli, I think we had better lay down some ground rules—'

'The first one being that you call me Wolf and I will call you Angel. I thought we were both agreed that we do not want to cause Stephen any concern at this time?' he pressed, as she would have once again protested at his familiarity.

Her mouth firmed. 'If I really were the gold-digger you have assumed me to be, then do you really think I would actually care about that?'

Wolf's dark brown eyes hardened warningly. 'I think that for the duration of Stephen's incapacity it is in your best interests to continue to appear the dutiful and loving daughter.'

Angelica paled slightly at the deliberate threat she could hear in Wolf's tone. 'And what part are *you* going to play, Count Gambrelli?' she scorned.

'Me?' he echoed derisively. 'In Stephen's presence I will continue to be the caring and considerate friend I have always been.'

'And when we're alone?' Angelica breathed softly.

'I believe that is yet to be decided,' he answered provocatively.

Angelica eyed him warily. Wolf Gambrelli, she already knew, was dangerous with a capital D!

But she stood her ground as he took a step towards her, and their gazes clashed in challenge as he stood only inches away from her.

So close she could once again see the gold flecks in the chocolate-brown of his eyes...

So close she felt a quiver of awareness down her spine at the intent in his body language...

So close that she was aware of every inch of his powerfully muscled physique...

So close that her eyes became locked on the slight cruelty that edged those finely sculptured lips.

She took a deep breath. 'I'm really not what you think I am, Wolf.'

He smiled mirthlessly. 'No?'

'No,' she sighed.

He shrugged his broad shoulders. 'Only time will tell whether that is true or not. But I believe you were about to mention some ground rules, for the time we are living together...?'

He was being deliberately provocative, Angelica knew. They wouldn't be 'living together' in the sense he implied—only sharing a house. Considering that Stephen's house in London was a twelve-bedroomed mansion, they didn't even have to *see* each other while they were both staying there if they didn't want to!

And caution—self-preservation!—told Angelica that she didn't want to be anywhere near this man if she could help it.

'I think while we are both staying at Stephen's

house, the further we stay away from each other the better it will be for both of us,' Angelica announced.

Wolf noted the slight pallor to her cheeks, the slight tremble of her sensuously full lips, that her throat moved convulsively as she swallowed and her breathing was agitated. Then his eyes were drawn once more to her breasts, and he easily recalled the deep rosy hue of her nipples, how she had tasted earlier today when he'd kissed and suckled her.

His body hardened just thinking about how good she had felt and tasted, telling him that staying away from this woman when he desired her so much was not an option!

Not a viable one, at least…

'What else?' he prompted.

She pulled a face. 'I don't think there need be any other rules if we stick to that one.'

'But, Angel—'

'Except that one!' she repeated determinedly. 'I really cannot accept you using Stephen's term of affection for me.'

Wolf arched dark blond brows. 'You don't think I can be affectionate…?'

She thought this man could be whatever he chose to be if he wanted something badly enough!

'Affectionate, maybe. But I don't believe you

have ever been in love with any of the women you've been involved with!' she scorned.

Wolf's face became shuttered. 'If I had, then we would not be having this conversation.'

Angelica looked puzzled. 'What do you mean...?'

He smiled without humour. 'The men in my family—those of us who are still bachelors, anyway—have come to call it the Gambrelli Curse.'

'I don't understand...'

Wolf explained. 'Simply put, Angel, if I had ever been in love, then I would now be married to the woman I loved—no doubt with a dozen children to show for that love!'

'So? I still don't understand,' Angelica persisted.

'No, I don't suppose you do,' he accepted wearily. 'But it is no secret that the men in my family love only once in their lifetime,' he continued. 'Completely. Totally. With an all-consuming passion.'

Her eyebrows raised in disbelief. 'But that's—'

'It is as much a fact as your own father,' Wolf rasped. 'The men of the Gambrelli family, once smitten, love for a lifetime. My grandfather fell in love with my grandmother when the two of them were only children together, and my grandfather was as devoted and as much in love even after almost seventy years of marriage. My father met and fell for my mother when he was almost fifty and she was only twenty-five, but it was a love that lasted for all of his life. Such a deep and devoted love that my mother, despite being still beautiful and charming, has remained a widow since his death ten years ago. My Uncle Carlo, my cousin Cesare's father, fell in love with the family's maid forty years ago—a match the family did not approve of—but my uncle defied family disapproval and married her anyway. She died when Cesare and his sister were only children, at which point my uncle slowly drank himself to death. Now my cousin Cesare loves his wife Robin in that same all-consuming way,' he concluded.

'And is he unhappy with that love…?' Angelica asked softly; in the photographs she had seen of Cesare Gambrelli and his new wife, the couple had always looked ecstatically happy together.

'Not in the least,' Wolf acknowledged ruefully. 'In fact, he is happier than I have ever seen him. But he is not the man I knew before he met Robin,' he added.

Angelica couldn't see that being a bad thing; as far as she remembered, the Cesare Gambrelli she had read about in the newspapers before his marriage had apparently been a cold, hard man, interested only in concluding his next business deal and bedding his next woman.

A man very much like Wolf himself, in fact...

'So, to answer your question, Angel,' Wolf went on, 'no, I have never been in love. In fact, I have spent the whole of my thirty-six years avoiding it!'

And he intended going on avoiding it, if the hard decisiveness of his tone was anything to go by!

Which suited her just fine; she didn't want to fall in love with this man either...

'I believe you mentioned going to see your cousin's baby today?' she reminded him pointedly.

Wolf guessed this was Angel's way of getting him to leave. 'After talking with Stephen I'm in no hurry now,' he replied. 'In fact, I think you will come to know that on certain occasions my—self-control is infinite,' he murmured challengingly, knowing she was aware of his double meaning as her complexion pinkened.

The dismay he had felt earlier at Stephen's request that he look after Angel while the other man was in hospital no longer existed now that Wolf knew she was Stephen's illegitimate daughter rather than his mistress.

In fact, sharing a house with this woman—a woman Wolf only had to look at to desire her, could prove interesting.

Her misty grey eyes met his unflinchingly. 'I'm asking you to leave my bedroom, Count Gambrelli.'

'So it would appear.'

'Wolf, please just— What are you doing?' she gasped as one of his hands moved to cup the side of her face, his fingers tightening about her chin as she would have pulled away.

Wolf's eyes narrowed as he looked down at her searchingly.

Was this woman what she claimed to be?

The innocent result of an affair Stephen had obviously had with her mother twenty-seven years ago?

Or was Angel the opportunist, the gold-digger, that Wolf feared she might be?

Whatever she was, or was not, Wolf knew that he desired her—was aware that even now he wanted to kiss her, to touch her, to feel her silky nakedness against him as he caressed her to fevered desire, as those long slender hands caressed him to the same ecstasy.

His mouth tightened and he released her to step away from that temptation. Anticipation would only sharpen his desire for her.

'It has been decided that I will arrive at Stephen's town house in time for dinner tomorrow—Monday evening,' he told her flatly. 'In the meantime, I advise you not to—trouble Stephen with your reservations about the arrangement,' he added warningly.

Angelica blinked dazedly after he released her, so suddenly she almost staggered, very aware that Wolf had been on the point of kissing her again. The intent in his dark brown eyes had been unmistakable, as had the self-disgust seconds later as he'd thrust her impatiently away from him, her skin still tinglingly aware from just the touch of his fingers.

The situation of the two of them sharing a house for any length of time was intolerable.

Totally unacceptable.

And totally unchangeable if she wasn't to alarm and upset Stephen before he had the operation which could save his life…

She might not trust Wolf Gambrelli, but Stephen obviously did—had chosen the other man as a protector for her.

But with her own defences in tatters every time this man so much as touched her, who was going to protect her from Wolf Gambrelli…?

CHAPTER SIX

'How does Stephen seem to you?'

Angelica's fingers tightened on the metal balcony in front of her, but other than that she showed no outward sign that she was resentful of Wolf Gambrelli's intrusion into her few moments of peace before the hell of having him staying here with her at Stephen's London home began in earnest.

She had been in the drawing room with Stephen when Wolf had arrived at the house half an hour or so ago, and had excused herself as soon as she was able, on the pretext that she wanted to go upstairs and change before dinner.

But as she'd reached the gallery at the top of the wide staircase in the Georgian town house, the lure of children's laughter in the park across the road had been too much for her. She had opened one of the two sets of French doors to go outside on the balcony and look across to where the children were feeding the ducks and swans on the pond there. Wolf must have seen that open door and realised where she was.

'Seem to me?' she echoed, not bothering to turn and look at Wolf, knowing exactly how breathtakingly handsome he looked in a casual brown shirt and brown tailored trousers. The increase in her pulse-rate at just the thought of his broad expanse of powerful chest, tapered waist and muscled thighs told her that she didn't need to look at him to be totally aware of him!

Wolf knew women well enough to sense when he was being physically and mentally blocked out. He studied the slender line of Angel's back in a deep green tee shirt and faded denims that fitted snugly over the curve of her bottom and long slender legs. The long length of her hair was brushed back and secured in a ponytail, leaving wispy strands on her creamy forehead.

Wolf was *totally* aware of all her slender womanliness.

His eyes narrowed as she suddenly turned, her hands behind her as she leant back on the metal balcony, and met his gaze challengingly, her breasts thrust forward in the tight tee shirt, two bright wings of colour in the pallor of her cheeks. From annoyance? Or from something else…?

'How do you *expect* Stephen to seem this

evening, Wolf?' she said scathingly. 'He's going to have an operation tomorrow that may or may not give him another few years of life.' Her voice lowered. 'Or he may not survive the operation,' she added, before her chin rose determinedly. 'I didn't arrive myself until an hour or so ago, but I can see he's nervous, tense—he seems to me exactly like a man who might just have spent his last day on earth!'

Wolf's mouth tightened as he heard the tremor of emotion in her voice. 'Then it is up to the two of us to make sure that this evening is an enjoyable one for him.'

She eyed him suspiciously. 'Meaning?'

He sighed. 'Meaning that I suggest the two of us call a truce this evening—for Stephen's sake,' he declared.

'Like the ceasefire on Christmas Day in the trenches during the First World War?' Angel taunted.

Wolf gave a rueful smile. 'Well, I would suggest that we don't attempt to kill each other the following day—but, yes, that's exactly what I'm proposing.' He wasn't altogether sure that he liked the sudden gleam of possibility in her misty grey eyes—as if Angel didn't find the idea of killing him tomorrow such an unacceptable one!

'That sounds only sensible to me.' She gave her

terse agreement. 'Now, if you will excuse me, Count Gambrelli, I really do have to go and change before dinner…'

Wolf didn't move as she approached the doorway where he stood, his dark gaze hooded as she turned sideways to slip past him, the tips of those firm, uptilting breasts brushing lightly against his chest as she did so.

Angelica drew in a sharp breath as her body came into contact with Wolf's, her breasts seeming to visibly swell, her nipples hardening achingly to tingle with awareness.

She raised startled lids, her gaze instantly caught and held by eyes of deep chocolate, her breathing shallow, a nerve pulsing hotly in her throat as she stared up at those hard sculptured features, at the clenched jaw and the long, sensuous line of Wolf's mouth.

Just remembering that mouth against her breasts yesterday, the heated warmth within and the moist flick of his tongue against her hardened nipples, was enough to take her breath away.

She moistened her lips with the tip of her tongue, and then realised what a bad idea that had been as Wolf followed that movement, at the same time as his own tongue moved across the firm nobility of his own lips; it was almost as if it was his tongue on her lips—as if he were the one touching, tasting her.

The ache in her breasts increased painfully, making them feel heavy, laden, and her back slightly arched involuntarily as she longed for that ache to be appeased.

Wolf's breath caught in his throat as he saw the longing in those misty grey eyes. His head was already starting to lower towards hers when she suddenly broke eye contact, her long lashes lowering as she dipped her head before taking the sideways step that took her into the house and out of his reach.

His hands clenched at his sides even as he breathed out with a shuddering sigh, his mouth tightening before he turned to look at her standing on the threshold of the French windows.

'How are your cousin's wife and daughter?' she paused to ask stiltedly.

'Well,' he replied. 'Thank you,' he added belatedly, having been thrown slightly by the polite enquiry.

As no doubt he had been meant to be! Angel obviously wasn't in the least comfortable with the total physical awareness that sprung up between the two of them every time they were together.

Wolf couldn't say he was too thrilled by it

himself. The fact that Angel had turned out to be Stephen's daughter rather than his mistress wasn't any more reassuring concerning her motives for being in Stephen's life. Certainly it hadn't helped lessen the sexual tension Wolf felt whenever he was in her company!

'This is their first child, isn't it...?' Angelica continued conversationally, self-consciously aware that she had given herself away a few minutes ago, that Wolf had been well aware of her arousal.

But she knew a little about Cesare Gambrelli; like Wolf, he and Wolf's brother, Luc Gambrelli, were often featured in the newspapers, who chronicled their affairs with one beautiful woman after another. In fact, the handsome Sicilians had been three of the most eligible bachelors in the world until Cesare had married the lovely Robin Ingram the previous year.

By all accounts happily surrendering to that 'Gambrelli Curse'!

Wolf nodded. 'They also have an adopted son called Marco.' He gave a smile. 'He isn't much more than a baby himself, so Robin is going to have her hands full. But after years of believing she would never have children I somehow don't think she's going to mind that,' he explained affectionately.

His fondness for his cousin and his wife was obviously genuine, although Angelica found Wolf taking on the role of family man as unbelievable as he obviously found it himself.

'You said you had only arrived a short time ago yourself…?' he prompted lightly.

Angelica looked at him, feeling confused. 'Sorry?'

Wolf elaborated. 'I know that Stephen spent the day tying up loose ends before his operation tomorrow—I was wondering how you had spent your day.'

From anyone else Angelica would have accepted that this was nothing but a polite query, as much a conversation-filler as her own query about his cousin's new baby. But she knew all too well that when they were alone, as they were now, Wolf Gambrelli never found any reason to be polite to her.

'I drove down to Kent to spend a few hours with my family,' she answered him slowly.

'Ah, yes—your mother, stepfather, and your two sisters,' he remembered.

And what was so wrong about that? Angelica wondered, even as she bristled at Wolf's derisive tone.

'I obviously won't be able to go and see them for a while once Stephen has his operation,' she defended.

'Obviously not,' Wolf agreed. 'I spent my afternoon at the office of Stephen's lawyer,' he informed her.

She blinked. 'You did...?'

'You are now officially his sole heir, with his lawyer and myself as executors.'

'I told you I never wanted that,' she reminded him sharply.

'Whether you want it or not, that is what you now are.'

Whether you want it or not...

Wolf didn't have to state it any more clearly than that; he obviously still thought her reasons for entering Stephen's life were suspect.

Her chin rose defensively. 'That doesn't mean I'm going to accept it. Should the worst happen.'

Blond brows rose over sceptical brown eyes. 'You're going to give Stephen's millions away to charity? Is that it?'

Angelica stiffened resentfully. 'Why not?'

She wouldn't know what to do with all that money anyway, and had never had any ambitions to be wealthy, let alone incredibly rich.

If the people she had met who were multimillionaires—namely, Stephen and Wolf—were anything to go by, then she didn't think extreme wealth had brought either of them happiness.

Stephen's marriage had been far from happy, his affairs transient. And Wolf, whether through choice or not, lived what she considered to be a lonely life—his very public affairs indicative of his decision not to involve himself in a permanent relationship.

To Angelica, the two men were the epitome of the saying 'money can't buy you happiness'. Their lives were undoubtedly made more comfortable by their extreme wealth, and they could obviously buy anything they wanted. But, having been brought up in a household where love was more important than money, Angelica didn't value being rich in the way that Stephen and Wolf did.

Wolf eyed Angel, sure that she wasn't seriously contemplating giving away all the wealth that Stephen had spent a lifetime accruing, positive she would change her mind once she knew just how big her bank balance would become!

If Stephen died…

His mouth hardened. 'This is, of course, a theoretical conversation.'

'It most certainly is!' Angel snapped.

Wolf nodded. 'I have every confidence that Peter Soames will ensure that everything goes well tomorrow; he's one of the leading heart surgeons in the world.'

'You checked?' Angel's brows rose.

'Of course,' Wolf confirmed dismissively.

His reputation for enjoying himself, and being involved with some of the most beautiful women in the world, might give the impression that he was just a European playboy, but he hadn't got to be so successful in the business world by not exercising the astuteness of his considerable intelligence.

'Of course,' Angel echoed dryly. 'Now I really should go and change for dinner,' she told him briskly. 'Stephen will be wondering what's delaying me.'

Wolf reached out to grasp her arm as she turned to walk away. Angel glanced down at that restraining hand before looking up at him enquiringly.

'Stephen loves you very much,' he told her tautly, his jaw clenched. 'I sincerely hope he isn't mistaken in that love.'

Angelica's mouth tightened at his obvious implication. 'I've told you before, Count Gambrelli. How Stephen and I feel about each other really isn't any of your business—'

'And your own family?' he cut in harshly. 'You said you've seen them today. How do they feel about all this?'

Angelica stiffened. 'Feel about it…?'

'It cannot have escaped their notice that you are all set to become a very wealthy woman—'

'Stop right there, Count Gambrelli!' she warned coldly, grey eyes glittering angrily. 'You are a typical example of how wealth can warp your perspective of people, making you constantly suspicious of the motives of others,' she accused, at the same time shaking off his hold on her arm. 'My family—my mother and stepfather and my two sisters—have no more interest in Stephen's wealth than I do!'

Wolf wished he could believe her. In fact, he wished that she was anyone other than who she really was. And that he desired her a little less...

'I hope you are right,' he responded abruptly.

'I am,' she assured him. 'Now, if you will excuse me...?'

'I will excuse you many things, Angel,' he told her. 'But hurting Stephen is not one of them,' he warned.

'That isn't going to happen!' she bit out.

'I hope not,' Wolf rejoined. 'And I meant what I said earlier.'

Angelica gave him a searching look. He had said so many things these last ten minutes that she no longer had any idea what he was referring to.

'I would like, for Stephen's sake, there to be a

truce between the two of us this evening,' he reminded her evenly.

He had just insulted her—yet again!

Had almost kissed her—yet again!

And yet he still expected her to be able to behave in front of Stephen this evening as if everything were friendly and relaxed between the two of them!

'I'll do my very best to pretend that I actually like you, Wolf,' she retorted.

He gave an arrogant inclination of his head. 'And I'm sure that your very best will be more than good enough…'

Angelica gave him a narrow-eyed glare. 'How about you, Wolf?' she challenged. 'Are you going to be able to pretend to like me, too?'

He let his eyes move once again over her form in lazy appraisal, starting at her hair, lingering over the flushed beauty of her face, before moving down the length of her body, slowly—oh-so-slowly!—over the pertness of her breasts, and then trailing a leisurely path down the flatness of her waistline to her curvaceous hips.

Angelica felt even more hot and uncomfortable when his hooded gaze finally returned to her face.

'Oh, but I do like you, Angel,' he finally murmured throatily. 'In fact, I more than like certain parts of you.'

'Unfortunately, Wolf, I come as a complete package!' Angelica replied through gritted teeth, too annoyed by his obvious insolence to even pick up on his familiarity with her name, and shooting him one last quelling glance before turning on her heel and marching off to her bedroom.

Three hours at most—that was all she had to get through this evening in the maddening Wolf Gambrelli's company. It promised to be three hours of torture…!

'Pick up eight cards, Wolf!' Stephen told the younger man with a triumphant laugh as he laid a black jack on top of the one Angelica had just put down.

Angelica gave a rueful smile as she watched the interplay between the two men. If anyone had told her a year ago that she would spend two hours after dinner playing children's card games with Stephen   Foxwood and Wolf Gambrelli, two of the most notorious womanisers in the world, then she wouldn't have believed them!

But that was exactly what the three of them had done. With not enough people to make up a bridge four, or for any other adult card game they could think of, Angelica had been forced to fall back on her memory of the card games she'd used to play with her parents and sisters when she was a child.

To her surprise, the two men had actually seemed to enjoy the last couple of hours, the underlying light-hearted male rivalry between them spurring them on.

Although Angelica wasn't absolutely sure that seeing Wolf in this relaxed mood was an altogether good idea. She felt more aware of him than ever. The huskiness of his laugh seemed to move across her skin like a caress; the warmth in his chocolate-brown eyes, whenever he chanced to look at her, seemed to actually heat the blood in her veins.

Although it had to be said that, as a means of distracting Stephen from thoughts of tomorrow's operation, it had definitely succeeded. His earlier tension had completely evaporated as he and Wolf constantly vied to beat each other.

'Game over,' she announced, and placed her last card on the stack. 'And time for bed, too, I think,' she added lightly as she began to collect up the cards.

'Unfair,' Stephen cried protestingly. 'You've won the last four games!'

'I think Angel took advantage of our ignorance of the game and made the rules up as she went along,' Wolf concurred.

'Isn't that a woman's prerogative, Wolf?' Stephen asked him teasingly. 'And it's knowing that those rules can change at any time that keeps us men constantly on our toes!' he added. 'They learn it in the cradle, I think.'

Wolf smiled. 'Perhaps I should warn Cesare concerning his new daughter.'

'I wouldn't bother.' Stephen laughed. 'Believe me, he'll discover the truth of what I've said soon enough!'

'You are both talking absolute nonsense,' Angelica reproved.

Although, completely aware of Wolf's opinion of her, she somehow doubted that his remarks had been made as teasingly as Stephen's...

'You're right—it is time for bed.' Wolf spoke briskly now, standing up. 'I'll leave the two of you alone to talk for a while,' he announced, before leaving.

Angelica watched him go, her gaze drawn to the lean length of his body as he moved with that unconsciously predatory elegance. Having changed into a black evening suit before coming down to dinner, his shirt snowy-white and teamed with a red bow-tie, this evening he looked more lethally elegant—and more disturbing!—than usual.

'He's a good man, Angel,' Stephen told her.

Angelica turned back to him, her expression deliberately bland; 'good' wasn't a term she would ever have used where Wolf Gambrelli was concerned. Under any circumstances!

'I'm sure you're right,' she answered noncommittally, not willing to get into conversation about a man Stephen considered his closest friend, but who she considered more sexually dangerous than any man she had ever met.

Stephen put one of his hands over hers. 'You can trust him, Angel,' he assured her, his gaze searching. 'Although you don't seem too sure of that…?' he probed concernedly.

She swallowed hard, not wanting to lie, but not wanting to worry Stephen unduly either. 'Wolf and I really don't know each other very well yet,' she admitted, knowing that if she had her way they wouldn't get to know each other at all!

Stephen gave a smile. 'And I'm sure that what you do know about Wolf—what you've read about him in the press—doesn't exactly imbue you with confidence!' He chuckled. 'But I can assure you that there's much more to Wolf than that international playboy image they like to project onto him.' He sobered. 'He's a good son to Alethea. A protective big brother to Luc. And he's been a good friend to me over the years. As I know he will be to you, too, if you will let him,' he finished softly.

'I'm sure that you're right,' Angelica reassured her father. 'But it's you we should be talking about, not Wolf.' She looked at him sympathetically. 'Are you okay about tomorrow?'

He gave her hand a squeeze before leaning back in his chair. 'I'm as ready as I'm ever going to be,' he told her. 'Which isn't saying much!' he grimaced. 'I've never liked doctors or hospitals. Wouldn't have the guts to go through with this at all if it weren't for you. I'll pull through, Angel,' he said. 'With you waiting for me when I come round after the anaesthetic, I have every reason in the world to survive this,' he decided determinedly. 'And even if I don't—'

'Please don't talk like that,' Angelica choked, turning her hand so that she grasped his now. 'I couldn't bear it if anything happened to you!' And she knew it was the truth.

They had come very late to this father-daughter relationship, but she already knew that it would leave a huge emotional vacuum in her life if anything were to happen to Stephen now.

He gave her an encouraging smile. 'Angel, no matter what happens, this last year of knowing you, of having you as my daughter, has been the best year of my life.'

She blinked back the tears that threatened to fall, knowing that she had to remain strong—that Stephen needed her to be strong right now.

'We're going to have a lot more years together yet,' she declared.

'I hope so,' he agreed. 'Now, it really is time you got off to bed,' he chided briskly. 'I still have a few things I need to do before going up myself.'

More last-minute things he needed to do before his operation tomorrow, Angelica knew, and she made her way slowly up to her bedroom, feeling incredibly lonely at this moment. She wished she could have her family around her to turn to, but knew in the circumstances that wasn't impossible. It simply wouldn't do to have her mother—Stephen's ex-lover from long ago—or either of her two sisters—no relation to Stephen whatsoever—with her right now. Which meant she had to—

She came to a halt as she turned down the hallway that led to her bedroom and saw Wolf standing there.

She looked at him warily. What did he want now? Had he waited for her to come to bed in order to issue more last-minute warnings? More threats? If so—

'I wanted to make sure everything was all right before I went to bed,' he responded, as if in answer to her question. 'That there have been no last-minute…problems.'

Angelica blinked at his words, frowning slightly as her wariness deepened.

Wolf saw the emotions flickering across the beautiful transparency of her face as she stood several feet away from him: her obvious surprise at finding him waiting here, quickly followed by wariness.

He gave a rueful smile. 'We have called a truce for this evening, remember?' he reminded her almost teasingly as he straightened.

Her frown remained, as did the wariness in her misty grey eyes, as she lifted her chin slightly defensively. 'I thought that was only for Stephen's benefit…?'

'Did you?' Wolf prompted. 'You would rather that the two of us returned to hostilities now?'

In truth, he wasn't completely sure why he *had* waited for her here—other than that it had suddenly occurred to him as he came up the stairs a short time ago that if her feelings towards Stephen were genuine—*if* they were—she might be upset after she and Stephen had said goodnight for the evening, and in need of that protection Stephen wished him to give to her.

If her feelings for Stephen were genuine…

'No, of course not,' she replied heavily. 'I just—It's all so—' She shook her head and shut her eyes against the tears that were threatening again.

Wolf took a step towards her. 'You have to be strong now, Angel,' he told her quietly. 'For Stephen's sake as well as your own.'

'But what if he doesn't survive, Wolf?' she cried emotionally, her eyes misting with tears now. 'What if it all goes horribly wrong—?' She broke off as Wolf gathered her in his arms to pull her tightly up against him, his chin resting on the silky darkness of her hair as she laid her head against his chest, her arms tightly about his waist as she clung to him. 'I don't think I could bear it if anything happened to him!' she acknowledged chokingly, the heat of her tears dampening his evening shirt.

Much as he tried, Wolf couldn't remain immune to her pain. His Italian sense of honour, his own concern for Stephen, made it impossible for him to withstand the appeal of her scalding grief.

He let her cry for a minute or so before speaking. 'Nothing is going to happen to Stephen,' he assured her gently.

Angel shook her head, wispy tendrils of her hair brushing against his chin. 'We don't know that,' she sobbed.

'No,' he conceded. 'But we can be assured that everything that can be done most certainly will.'

'I know.' She sighed. 'I just—'

'We mustn't let Stephen see you like this,' Wolf ordered, even as he took one arm from about her and reached out to open the door to her bedroom. 'Come, Angel,' he encouraged, and he turned her towards the open doorway, his arm still supportive about the slenderness of her waist. 'We should at least get out of the hallway, in case Stephen should come upstairs to bed.'

Although he wasn't sure going into Angel's bedroom with her was a good idea.

Not for her.

But for Wolf himself.

Because just holding her in his arms like this, aware of every soft curve of her body, was enough to arouse the desire in him that seemed never far below the surface whenever he was around this particular woman…

CHAPTER SEVEN

ANGELICA snapped into awareness of exactly where she was—and who she was with!—as she heard her bedroom door close softly behind them.

Just because Wolf was actually being nice to her for a change, it didn't alter the fact that he didn't trust her, or her motives for being in Stephen's life.

Neither did it change the fact that she was attracted to Wolf's sensual magnetism—in spite of the suspicions he maintained about her!

She moved his arm, which was draped about her waist, away from her, and released herself from the heat of his body to turn and look at him from beneath lowered lashes. 'Thank you for your—concern just now, Wolf.' She spoke guardedly. 'But, as we all have a difficult day ahead of us tomorrow, I think it's time we went to bed now. Alone. In our respective bedrooms,' she emphasised, as she saw the way his chiselled lips slowly curved into a smile.

'I somehow had a feeling that you wouldn't be inviting me to join you here,' he commented.

Her chin tilted. 'Then you weren't disappointed, were you?' she came back, their truce definitely over as far as she was concerned. This man was far too threatening when he was being nice to her!

Wolf kept his expression deliberately bland, at the same time aware that Angel still looked beautiful—even with the trace of tears still visible on her cheeks.

The grey knee-length dress she wore was a perfect foil for her magnolia complexion and for the darkness of her hair as it swung loosely about her shoulders and down the length of her spine, and those misty grey eyes were dark from spent emotion.

In the same way they had darkened when he had kissed her yesterday morning…!

A memory that had continued to haunt him since…

He still didn't know this woman well enough to tell whether her feelings for Stephen were genuine or not—although after her upset just now he was starting to believe that maybe they were. But his wariness of her certainly didn't seem to stop his body from responding to the allure of her sensuously curving body every time he was anywhere near her.

'I have a feeling, Angel,' he said throatily, 'that in certain—areas I wouldn't find you disappointing at all!'

Angelica's eyes narrowed warningly even as she felt warmth enter her cheeks. 'What a pity you'll never be in a position to find out!'

'No?' Wolf returned softly. 'That depends what position you had in mind.'

The warmth deepened in her cheeks at his deliberate provocation. 'With you?' she scorned. 'No position whatsoever,' she assured him confidently. 'We had to be polite to each other this evening for Stephen's sake, Wolf,' she reminded him. 'Let's not either of us imagine there's any more to it than that.'

Wolf looked totally relaxed as he easily countered her remark. 'But the imagination can be a wonderful thing, Angel,' he told her. 'For instance, since yesterday morning I've been imagining what it would be like to—'

'It really is late, Wolf,' Angelica cut in, since what had happened between them yesterday morning was something she would rather forget. Or at least put firmly to the back of her mind. Something she couldn't do when Wolf was so close to her.

And she was tired of telling him she didn't

like him using that shortened version of her name—especially the way Wolf said it, almost like a caress…

'—go riding with you again,' he finished, as if she hadn't spoken, looking at her intently.

Angelica drew in a sharp breath at his deliberately provocative tone, her eyes sparkling with temper now. 'I never ride when I'm in London,' she snapped.

Wolf had no idea why he was deliberately being such a bastard. Except that he resented his earlier concern for and now his physical response to this woman. But was that her fault? When all was said and done, Angel had done very little to actually encourage him. In fact the opposite, if anything.

'Pity,' he drawled as he straightened. 'I'll leave you to your lonely bed, then.'

'And you to yours,' she came back brittly.

Wolf paused with his hand on the doorknob. 'If you should change your mind…'

'I won't,' Angel assured him. 'I've already told you. I have no interest in the sort of transient relationship that is all a man like you has to offer—' She broke off, impatient with her own candour as she saw his gaze narrow dangerously. 'It really is late, Wolf,' she repeated insistently, walking over to the door.

He let out a sharp breath, having been stung once again by her comment about a man like him. Another man like Stephen was what she meant. Her father, the married man who'd had an affair with Angel's mother twenty-seven years ago and unknowingly created a baby. But there were subtle differences between himself and Stephen that Angel refused to recognise.

For reasons that weren't his fault, Stephen had been trapped into a marriage that had ultimately brought him no physical satisfaction. His relationship with Grace, after several dangerous failed pregnancies, had become more of a friendship than a loving marriage. Whereas Wolf had never even come close to marrying, knowing from his family history that when or if he did it would be a lifetime commitment to the woman he loved.

What Angelica didn't know was that his relationships with women weren't always of a physical nature. Several of the women he had dated or escorted over the years had stayed friends and nothing more.

And he had never, ever allowed any woman—physically involved with him or not—to assume that he would ultimately be interested in marriage.

But, given the strength of her feelings, these

were subtleties that, even if he were to point them out, he doubted Angel would appreciate.

Did it actually matter that she wouldn't appreciate his side of the story?

It didn't. It just rankled to be placed in the same category as the man that Stephen had perhaps necessarily become during his married life.

'I will wish you goodnight, then, Angel,' he said brusquely, before letting himself out of the bedroom.

A good night? Angelica echoed to herself, as she continued to look at the closed bedroom door. Worrying about Stephen had already meant that she would spend a restless night; now this last conversation with Wolf totally ensured that she wouldn't sleep.

She had thought she knew what type of man Wolf was—selfish, egotistical, totally cavalier in his relationships with women. And yet the fact that he had waited for her to come up to bed after her talk with Stephen, that Wolf had actually been concerned for her wellbeing, seemed to imply there was more to him than that.

The last thing she wanted to do was actually start to *like* Wolf Gambrelli!

Knowing that she was physically attracted to him—a physical attraction she had to constantly fight against, was bad enough without that!

* * *

'Take Angel for a coffee or something, Wolf,' Stephen advised his friend the next morning, as both men observed Angel's face paling. On the dot of eleven o'clock, medical personnel had come to collect Stephen to take him down to the operating theatre.

'Go for a walk in the park—anything. Just get her out of here for a few hours,' he ordered, as Angel continued to cling to his hand.

'Oh, but—'

'Stephen is right, Angel,' Wolf told her with kindly firmness as he reached out to touch her arm. 'It will be several hours before Peter Soames can tell us anything, and we may as well spend those hours not hanging around here.'

Not that this private clinic wasn't bright and airy, and the staff very attentive; Wolf just agreed with Stephen that it would do Angel no good to spend the waiting hours sitting here, fretting about the outcome of the operation.

He had been concerned by Angel's appearance when she'd joined him in the breakfast room earlier this morning. The make-up she had applied had done nothing to hide the dark smudges under her eyes from what had obviously been a sleepless night. In fact, no amount of make-up could have hidden the strain in her face as she'd refused all offers of food and drunk only a cup of coffee instead.

It had been a warning to Wolf that, once again, he might have made a serious error of judgement where Angel's feelings for Stephen were concerned.

And if that was the case, then he knew that some of his remarks to her during the last couple of days had been unnecessarily cruel.

Now, he maintained his hold on Angel's arm as he turned to the older man. 'We will both see you in a few hours, Stephen,' he said sincerely, hoping that was true. Stephen and he had been friends for so long now that he couldn't imagine the world without the other man's larger-than-life presence in it.

Stephen's eyes gleamed his appreciation. 'You most certainly will.' He shook the hand that Wolf held out to him before turning to hug Angel.

Angelica clung to Stephen now that the moment had come for him to go to Theatre. 'I want you to know that I love you!' she told him fervently, aware that it was the first time she had told him that, but knowing that she spoke the truth.

She hadn't been sure what to expect when she had decided to seek Stephen out a year ago—hadn't known what she would feel for him once they had met, or he for her. She had only known that he at least deserved to know that he had a daughter.

But his love for her, once he'd known who she was, had been instant—an outpouring that had been unconditional as he'd invited her totally into his life, allowing her to get to know him and encouraging her to love him in return.

That she could lose him without having told him how she felt was totally unacceptable to her.

'I love you too, Angel,' Stephen assured her emotionally. 'Wolf?' He looked up at the younger man appealingly.

Angelica didn't resist as Wolf took a determined grip on her shoulders to hold her firmly in front of him as the two of them watched Stephen being wheeled out of his room.

Just as she didn't resist when Wolf turned her in his arms and held her tightly against him as she felt the scalding tears once again cascading down her cheeks.

Neither did she raise any objections when, minutes later, his arm still about her shoulders, Wolf guided her from the clinic and outside into the bright sunshine.

Of where they went once they were actually outside Angelica had little recollection later. The next hours passed for her as if in a dream—

although she did vaguely remember drinking the cup of coffee Wolf offered her, and some time later eating a sandwich at his insistence.

But her stomach began to tie itself up in knots, making her regret eating that sandwich, as they made their way back to the clinic four hours later, her tension becoming almost unbearable as she wondered what awaited them there.

Wolf, having maintained a light and friendly conversation about heaven knows what during their absence from the clinic, could only applaud Stephen's decision to ask him to watch over Angel; left to her own devices, Wolf felt sure that she would simply have sat in the waiting room, falling more and more under the weight of her own dire imaginings, if he hadn't taken charge of the situation.

His own worries over Stephen's future he had kept firmly under control, knowing that Angel's need for emotional support was much deeper than his own.

The more he reflected, the more he realised he had indeed made a mistake about her motives for seeking Stephen out after Grace died.

After the insults and accusations he had hurled at her on Sunday and Monday, even after he'd known exactly who and what she was, it wasn't a

comfortable admission for him to have to make…
especially to himself!

But that didn't lessen the desire he knew he
already felt for her.

In fact, it made the clamouring of his senses
worse, leaving him with no defences against the
pull of her undoubted beauty and the warmth and
sincerity of her personality.

Not a good idea when he knew he was already
so physically aroused by her.

After years of remaining heart-free, of relish-
ing that freedom to the full—of avoiding the
Gambrelli Curse!—even the possibility that he
might be more than just attracted to Angel was
complete anathema to him!

His mouth tightened determinedly as he opened
the clinic door for her to enter. 'I'm sure there
should be some news of Stephen's condition by
now,' he suggested.

Or not, Angelica acknowledged frowningly, her
feet slowing as she almost felt a reluctance to find
out what that news was. She didn't know what she
would do, what she would say, if the operation
hadn't been a success—

'Angelica!'

She looked up gladly—disbelievingly!—as
she recognised that voice, her eyes widening as

her mother hurried from the waiting room, where she had obviously been sitting, to hurry down the carpeted corridor to where Angelica had come to a halt.

'Mum…?' she voiced dazedly.

'I decided I couldn't let you go through this on your own, darling,' her mother told her emotionally as they hugged. 'Neil and I discussed it and decided, despite the awkwardness of the situation—' she gave a rueful smile '—that I should come and be with you this morning, at least. Only I was told by the nursing staff when I arrived that Count Gambrelli had taken you out for a few hours…' She looked curiously at the man who stood slightly behind Angelica.

At Wolf.

Angelica's cheeks regained some of their colour. She knew exactly what her mother would see as she looked at Wolf: a tall, golden-haired man, his olive-skinned complexion telling of his Italian heritage, his chiselled features devastingly handsome and telling of his lineage, his leanly muscled body lazily powerful in a casual cream shirt and faded denims.

She was also totally aware that she hadn't so much as mentioned Wolf's existence when she'd visited her family yesterday.

But what could she have told them? That Stephen's closest friend, a certain Count Gambrelli, had been asked to act as her protector over the next few days? That would only have led to her family asking any number of questions about him—questions Angelica would rather not answer…

Wolf's gaze narrowed as he looked at Angelica's mother—at the woman who had undoubtedly been Stephen's lover twenty-seven years ago.

Despite the twenty or so years' difference in their ages, the likeness between Angelica and her mother was unmistakable: both of them had that midnight-black hair—styled at a youthful shoulder-length on the older woman—and both were incredibly beautiful, possessed of the same misty grey eyes. Each was slender, and yet at the same time temptingly curvaceous in faded denims and fitted tee shirts.

No wonder Stephen had been in absolutely no doubt a year ago that Angelica was indeed his daughter by the woman who had been his lover so long ago!

'Mrs Harper.' He stepped forward to hold out his hand in greeting. 'I am Wolf Gambrelli. A close friend of Stephen's. He asked me to be with Angel today,' he added by way of explanation, as she still looked blank concerning his identity.

'Count Gambrelli,' she greeted him, with the same husky tones as Angelica, her hand briefly small and light against his. 'I can't tell you how much I appreciate your being here,' she added gratefully.

Angelica was still totally stunned at seeing her mother here—but not so taken aback that she couldn't see the speculative curiosity in her mother's expression, and her raised brows as she turned back to look at her daughter.

But what could she say about Wolf that wasn't obvious at first glance? That his rugged good-looks made him absolutely irresistible? That he was possessed of a subtle self-confidence that only the rich and successful seemed able to achieve?

Nevertheless, she felt some sort of explanation was probably necessary. 'Mum, I—'

'Miss Harper…?'

Angelica turned sharply at the sound of that quietly light tone, her gaze anxious on Peter Soames' face as she saw him standing a short distance away, still wearing the scrubs he had put on for the operation.

The entirely confident smile he gave her was enough to make her knees weaken as she realised that Stephen's procedure had to have been a success.

Wolf stood by as Angel turned instinctively to

her mother, the two women falling into each other's arms as they both burst into tears of relief.

Yes, he had indeed made a mistake—about Angel's family's feelings for Stephen as well as her own, Wolf acknowledged grimly.

Effectively removing his only defence against his own increasingly forceful emotions where Angel was concerned...

CHAPTER EIGHT

'WHAT are you doing?' Angelica questioned sleepily, as she felt herself being lifted up into strong arms.

She was exhausted from all the emotion of the last twelve hours, and the trauma of waiting for news of the outcome of Stephen's operation.

Not to mention the surprise—happily—of having found her mother waiting for her when she returned to the clinic with Wolf after their morning doing she had no idea what.

Then there had been the absolute relief when the surgeon, Peter Soames, had come to tell them that the operation had been the complete success they had all prayed it would be.

Plus the tearful reunion with Stephen when he'd returned to his room some time later, still slightly groggy from the anaesthetic, but aware enough to smile reassuringly at Angelica and Wolf before he'd fallen back into a drug-induced sleep.

Angelica's mother had decided to leave shortly after that, reassured by Wolf's presence.

A presence in which Angelica didn't share her mother's faith, now her worry over Stephen had abated!

Just as she didn't feel reassured now, as she felt Wolf lifting her up out of her the chair in Stephen's room, where she'd fallen asleep. Wolf took her into his arms against the powerful strength of his chest. 'What are you doing?' she queried again.

She could see the harsh lines of his face despite the muted lighting in Stephen's room.

She had absolutely refused to go back to the house when Wolf had suggested it earlier, insisting that she stay with Stephen during the night, stubbornly sitting herself in a chair at his bedside. She hadn't listened when Wolf had tried to persuade her otherwise. Wolf, after seeing her determined expression, had obviously decided he wasn't leaving either, and he'd folded his long length down on the chair opposite.

Which had made Angelica nerve-tinglingly aware of his broodingly silent presence, and she'd felt herself, rather than Stephen, to be the focus of the Sicilian's hooded brown gaze.

Although somewhere in the last half an hour or

so she must have relaxed—or, probably more correctly, been exhausted enough to actually fall asleep!

Wolf glanced down at her briefly as he strode with her in his arms across the room. 'Surely that's obvious?' he drawled.

'Not to me,' Angelica responded.

'A chair is not a comfortable place for you to sleep,' Wolf answered her. 'And, as you seem so determined to stay here tonight, I have organised the use of an adjoining room.'

The room next to Stephen's had been occupied by a middle-aged woman earlier today, Angelica recalled. Although no doubt if you were the charming but forceful Count Wolf Gambrelli, a little obstacle like that could easily be overcome.

She craned her neck to look worriedly at Stephen. But he still slept, despite the drip in his arm and the monitors around him that bleeped and buzzed softly in the silence.

'I'll leave the door slightly open, so that you can hear Stephen if he should waken and call for you,' Wolf informed her as he saw Angel's anxious glance at her father. 'If you are to be of any use to Stephen tomorrow you really need to have a comfortable night's sleep in a bed, rather than an uncomfortable nap in a chair,' he opined, and he carried her through to the accommodation next door, where only a glimmer of light from Stephen's room disturbed the darkness.

His plan had seemed perfectly logical to him earlier, when he'd organised this bedroom so that Angel could sleep more comfortably. But now, with her so warm and deliciously pliant in his arms, with her heady perfume awakening all his senses, and with a convenient bed on which to lay her, Wolf was no longer so sure of that logic!

Especially as, having lain her down on top of the soft bedding, instead of releasing her at he had intended, he instead found himself tempted to lie down beside her.

It was a temptation he was unable to resist as she looked up at him with misty grey eyes that were still slightly unfocused from her nap. The pouting softness of her slightly parted lips was an invitation he could hardly resist, either.

After spending hours in her company—hours when Wolf had been totally aware of the warm allure of her body, the clinging tee shirt doing little to hide the fact that her breasts were unconfined beneath its thin material, her bottom nicely rounded against her fitted denims—he knew that he had to touch her, to taste her. He *needed* to do those things.

He gathered her up close against him and then

laid his long length beside her on the bed, holding her tightly against him as his lips claimed hers lightly, searchingly, questioningly, sipping the taste of her as he asked for rather than demanded her response.

Angelica was too relaxed, too sleepy to protest as Wolf's mouth claimed hers once more. The mere fact that his lips roved gently rather than demandingly over hers was causing a thrill of exquisite pleasure to course through her body. He slowly drew her lower lip into his mouth, his tongue running delicately, teasingly, over the sensitised flesh. And she knew that she wanted him fully—completely.

But she was aware of where they were—of the muted but definite sounds of the clinic outside the privacy of their room—probably nurses as they quietly carried out their night-time duties. Softly she voiced her concern as Wolf's lips moved hypnotically across the sensitive line of her jaw.

'I locked the door,' he assured her distractedly.

'You did?' she murmured. 'That was very—sensible of you,' she added, sounding slightly dazed.

Wolf raised his head to look down at her, his eyes gleaming darkly in the dimly lit room. 'Being sensible was not the driving emotion behind my actions,' he said wryly.

She smiled dreamily. 'Shall I take a guess on what was?'

'I would rather show you,' he responded sensuously, his hands cradling each side of her face as he looked down at her before once again lowering his head to hers.

Her arms moved up about his shoulders, reacting instinctively in the anonymity of the semi-darkened room. Her fingers laced in the silkiness of the hair at his nape, her lips parting beneath his as he groaned low in his throat before deepening the kiss. He claimed her mouth, his tongue invading searchingly, and then he laid leisurely siege, possessing her with long, stroking, marauding movements.

Heat filled her. Her nipples engorged as they firmed, and the secret area between her thighs dampened hotly as Wolf moved his mouth from hers to seek out the hollows of the creamy column of her throat. His lips were demanding as they lingered at the heated throb of the pulse that beat there so erratically now.

Angelica's back arched instinctively as one of his hands moved to cup the fullness of her breast, curving, capturing, before his thumb slid caressingly over its hardened tip. At the same time his lips continued their leisurely exploration of her throat, his tongue seeking and finding all the delicate hollows as he trailed open-mouthed kisses down her creamy skin to where his hand cradled the breast that was ready and waiting for capture and ravishment.

She gasped as he drew her nipple inside his mouth to suckle and lave, his tongue erotically sensual through the thin material of her tee shirt, and her hands contracted in the thick silkiness of his hair as pleasure surged through her body in fiery waves.

She cried out as he drew her nipple deeply into his mouth, his tongue a rough rasp now, his teeth gently biting, driving her higher, ever higher. He shifted slightly and she could feel the hardness of his arousal against the waiting softness of her thighs.

Wolf moved against her once, twice, letting her know how badly he wanted her, that he was as aroused and needy as she was, before lifting his head slightly and pushing her tee shirt up above her breasts. His sight was accustomed to the semi-darkness now, and he looked down at the creamily tempting orbs, at the inviting hardness of those rose-tinted tips.

'Wolf…?' Angel groaned questioningly.

He raised his desire-darkened gaze to look at her—at the pouting fullness of lips swollen from his kisses, at her hair a dark swathe on the pillow beneath her, her grey eyes misted with arousal.

He continued to look into her eyes until, with his hand still laying claim to the breast that had already received his worshipping attention, he slowly lowered his head and turned his attention to her other breast. He kissed moistly across the milky swell, then to its side and beneath the firm uptilt, before moving his tongue lightly, teasingly, across the waiting nipple, watching Angel's face as she gave a surrendering sigh, her eyes closing as she arched against him in silent pleading.

It was a plea that Wolf answered as he suckled deeply—drinking, tasting—her heated response driving him to deeper intimacies. His other hand left her breast and trailed down the slenderness of her waist, easily dispensing with the button of her denims to slide the zip down and move in against her silky panties.

He could feel her heat, her dampness, through the silky material as his hand curved about her mound her thighs moved up to meet his caress.

His suckling at her breast grew less demanding as he centred her attention—and his—on the caress of his hand below, her raggedly indrawn breath, following by a quivering moan, telling him that he had succeeded. He left one last, lingering caress on her breast before moving up to once again claim her lips with his.

Her lips parted beneath his, the urgency of her kiss telling him of her need, of the aching desire his touch elicited as his fingers moved feather-light against her, allowing her to become accustomed to his touch before he moved assuredly beneath the silky scrap of material to her silken curls, and then inside to the heat he sensed—felt—throbbing hotly.

She was moist and swollen, so, so slick to the touch, becoming more so as he stroked against her, circling her entrance, the hardened nub above, and then back again as her thighs parted to allow him easier access.

Angelica lost herself in the sensual pleasure Wolf was creating with every touch, every caress, moving against him instinctively as he stroked his fingers lightly, and then harder, as he took his lips from hers and moved his free hand down her body to slide her denims and panties down her thighs before totally discarding them. Her eyes opened wide as she felt his hands on her hips, the touch of his lips against her sensitive inner thighs, and her breath left her in a gasp as she felt his tongue against her parted flesh.

Hot, aching pleasure engulfed her as he laved

her, before returning to her hardened nub, creating a rush of liquid fire between her thighs.

Her head moved from side to side on the pillow as she became lost in pleasure. Wolf's hands moved to cup her bottom as he lifted her to him, to gain further access, Angelica cried out, exquisite sensation coursing through her as she opened herself to his probing tongue, whimpering softly as she felt herself starting to spiral out of control.

Aware of her approaching release, Wolf gentled his tongue, holding her there, on the edge of what Angelica already knew was going to be an experience so shattering she might just lose her mind, as one of his hands moved once again to stroke her entrance. One finger moved enticingly around those swollen lips, almost penetrating, before once again retreating, repeating the caress until Angelica cried out for him to take her.

Wolf was totally aware of her need as he moved over her and then entered her slowly, assuredly, with his fingers. Angel's sheath tightened against him and, feeling the tremors that racked her body, he stroked rhythmically, her flesh so heated against him he knew he couldn't delay her climax for too much longer.

But still he held her on that peak of pleasure—wanting, needing to make her completely his, to lay claim to *all* of her hot, pulsing flesh. Still moving his fingers inside her, he moved his other hand slowly up the length of her body to once again capture her breast, drawing the nipple into his mouth, suckling hard, feeling her response as she became even slicker against his probing digits, her back arching as she moved up to meet his increasing thrusts.

When he was sure she could wait no longer, when he knew that she was beyond the point of no return, he moved once again, sliding down her body to flick his tongue compellingly against the hardened nub just above the thrust of his fingers once, twice, hearing her cry out even as he felt the convulsions of her orgasm, as her muscles clasped and shuddered about him, her release complete and prolonged.

A long, long time later, it seemed, Angelica drifted back down to complete awareness, able to taste the slight salt of her own tears on her cheeks. Not of sadness or regret, but of exquisite pleasure. Such unselfish pleasure, given and shared. She knew that Wolf had given but not taken, that he was still giving to her as he soothed and steadied the uncontrollable trembling of her body with the light, calming caress of his passionate hands.

This was *Wolf,* she told herself wonderingly.

The man she had accused not once but several times of being nothing but a love-them-and-leave-them womaniser.

But she knew now—beyond any doubt—that if that were truly what he was, then none of those women in his past had ever gone away feeling used by his attentions. That although Wolf might have no intention of giving his heart to any woman—of surrendering to the Gambrelli Curse of a lifetime of consuming love—he certainly gave everything else he had to give. Unreservedly, unselfishly.

Most of all unselfishly…

She stirred slightly in the arms he had wrapped about her as he once again moved to lie beside her and draw her close against him, his heart thumping loudly in his chest. 'Wolf—'

'No talking, Angel,' he chided gruffly.

'But I— You didn't—'

'I'm content,' he assured her softly. 'Angel, what happened just now was a celebration of life.'

He was right, Angelica realised. Wolf, out of relief that Stephen's operation had been successful, had aroused her to the pinnacle—as he'd said, to a celebration of life—and she—out of the same emotion?—had responded to that emotion, had known herself truly alive in his arms.

Wolf stirred restlessly against her. 'Let's not spoil our memory of this night with any soul-searching on my part or recriminations on yours,' he announced firmly.

'I wasn't going to do that, Wolf,' she assured him, knowing that there were no recriminations to make; Wolf had merely kissed her, making no attempt to force her into a response, and then waited until he knew she was completely willing in his arms before taking their lovemaking to another level.

A level Angelica had never known before—never even imagined before.

Oh, she'd had a relationship in the past—but not with a man like Wolf. And she had never known such earth-shattering pleasure before; her breasts were still highly sensitized, still hot and aching, and she was satisfied between her thighs in the aftermath of that hitherto unknown release.

No, there were no recriminations on her part to make; Wolf had pleasured her completely—had given but not taken.

And she could detect no signs of the self-satisfied male superiority she would have expected at his knowledge of the response he had drawn from her.

'Let's just accept this for what it was, hmm, Angel?' he prompted at her continued silence.

But what *was* it?

There was no doubting that Wolf was a wonderful lover, that he knew exactly how to give a woman pleasure. But was that 'celebration of life' all it had been?

Had Wolf just been the experienced lover that he always was, delivering satisfaction to the woman he currently held in his arms? Or had there been more to it than that?

She would be a fool, she knew, if she were to delude herself into thinking that there had been any more to what had happened between them just now than the giving and receiving of physical pleasure.

Did she want it to have been more than that?

Wolf was Stephen's counterpart—a man who undoubtedly enjoyed women. But, unlike Stephen, Wolf was also a man who never had made, and never would make, the commitment of loving a woman. And if Angelica expected any more from him than he had already given, then—like all those other women before her—she would merely be deluding herself.

No, she wouldn't fool herself—wouldn't make the mistake of imagining that their lovemaking meant anything to Wolf, that she meant any more to Wolf than all the other women he had known intimately over the years.

He had given, but so had she, with her uninhibited response, and Wolf had told her that he was content with that—that he didn't need anything else from her.

She turned more fully into his arms, snuggling comfortably against him beneath the sheet he had drawn up over the two of them, her head resting against his shoulder. The still rapid beat of his heart told her that even though he hadn't reached satisfaction himself, he had certainly been equally as aroused.

Quite how she was going to face him again in the morning, after he had explored her so intimately, when she had responded so fully, she had no idea. But that was something she would have to deal with then. Now she just wanted to fall asleep in his arms.

'Goodnight, Wolf,' she offered sleepily.

'Sleep, Angel,' he encouraged throatily.

She gave a contented sigh before closing her eyes and allowing the exhaustion she felt to steal over her.

Wolf realised Angel had fallen asleep as he felt her body relax fully against his and heard the even tenor of her breathing.

He drew in a ragged breath, forcing his own muscles to release as he held her lightly against him to lie back on the pillow and stare up at the ceiling, wide-eyed and sleepless, knowing that he hadn't been completely honest with her just now.

Oh, he was more than content with having loved Angel, with having felt, tasted her response, and knew that he could have continued to make love to her like that all night long and never tired of exulting in the way she gave of herself so completely.

But it was that very way she had of giving that scared the hell out of him!

He had known many women in his adult life—more women than he cared to remember. But they had been relationships based purely on physical desire, a mere exchange of gratification that both had found satisfying without any danger of emotional involvement.

He already knew that Angel was different from any of those women.

So different that he had shied away from having her touch and caress him, from the two of them making love completely. Because he had sensed that, with Angel, mere physical completion wouldn't be enough…

Because, he had to admit, there was already more between them than he had known with any other woman.

And he didn't want there to be…

CHAPTER NINE

ANGELICA woke slowly, slightly disorientated as she looked around the sunlit but unfamiliar room. Only the low murmur of voices in the adjoining room, Wolf and Stephen talking softly together, told her where she was and why.

And reminded her that last night Wolf had made thorough, exquisite love to her. Right here in this room. In this bed.

Oh, God…!

Last night she had put aside the repercussions of that intimacy as something to be dealt with in the morning. Well, now it *was* morning. She had to deal with it.

How?

Should she just pretend it had never happened? Or hope that Wolf would put her behaviour down to reaction—a celebration of life, as he had put it—much like that following a death? Culminating in the absolute relief of knowing Stephen's operation had been a success?

Would Wolf allow that? After learning her body, after kissing and touching her so intimately? Or would his mockery, his derision for her, only have increased?

Lying here debating the subject certainly wasn't going to give her any answers to those questions!

She threw back the covers to sit up and swung her legs to the floor, becoming aware that she no longer wore her jeans or her panties as she did so. Heated colour warmed her cheeks as she saw those two items of clothing neatly folded and placed on the chair beside the bed. Somewhere they certainly hadn't been the night before, after Wolf had slid them from her overheated body and thrown them to one side!

Angelica gave a firmly dismissive shake of her head as she hurriedly pulled on her clothes. She couldn't think of last night now. She wanted to go and see Stephen, to reassure herself that he really was going to be all right. In fact, she was slightly annoyed with Wolf that he hadn't woken her sooner.

The conversation stopped as she entered Stephen's room a minute or so later. The two men turned to look at her; Stephen looked lovingly pleased to see her, though, in contrast, Wolf's expression was blankly unreadable.

Even after last night, Angelica knew she couldn't expect *him* to be lovingly pleased to see her; love, as she already knew, didn't enter into Wolf's emotions.

In fact, she knew he wasn't pleased to see her, as he stood up slowly, his expression guarded and set with arrogantly distant hauteur.

She looked quickly away from those piercing brown eyes, the tearful brightness of her smile fixed totally on Stephen as she moved to clasp the hand he held out to her, before bending down to hug him as best she could around the hospital equipment with which he was still being monitored.

Wolf stood back, apart, as Angel sat on the side of Stephen's bed, the two of them talking softly together. He felt like something of an intruder at their emotional reunion, at the same time acknowledging that part of his awkwardness was due to the fact that, for the first time in his life, he had no idea how to deal with a situation.

Remembering making love to Angel last night—kissing her, caressing her, coming to know her body more intimately than he knew his own, her warmth, her physical generosity as she shared herself with him—had robbed him of his senses let alone his speech.

He had lain awake for hours last night, trying to decide what to do next.

His instincts told him to get as far away from Angel, from the temptation she was to him, as quickly as possible. His promise to Stephen—that he would act as Angel's protector while the other man remained in hospital—made that impossible.

He also recalled how he had held Angel in his arms, her hand resting trustingly on his chest as she remained cuddled against him for the whole of the night… A night during which Wolf hadn't slept at all as he tried to find some way out of this tangle.

Finally, he'd come to the conclusion that there wasn't one.

Except to keep Angel at a physical distance.

And that—despite his promise to Stephen—he certainly intended to do—because at this point in time the person Angel most needed protecting from was *him!*

'Take Angel back to the house for a while so that she can get something to eat and rest—Wolf…?' Stephen prompted softly as he sensed his distraction.

'Sorry.' He brightened, smiling self-derisively as he gave a shake of his head. 'I was miles away,' he dismissed lightly. 'You were suggesting that I take Angel back to the house for a while and ensure that she has something to eat before resting?'

Back to Stephen's house—where, apart from the unobtrusive staff, he would be completely alone with Angel...

But being alone with Angel was something that Wolf definitely wanted to avoid!

'There's no need for Wolf to take me any-where,' Angelica cut in impatiently as she saw Wolf's expression. 'I'm quite capable of taking myself back to the house. When I'm ready. Which I'm not,' she added stubbornly, as Stephen would have protested. She wasn't ready to find herself alone with Wolf just yet. Actually, she wasn't sure that she ever would be!

Her lover of last night—the man who had caressed her, kissed her, aroused her so sensu-ously, touched her so intimately—was totally missing this morning, Wolf looked every inch the arrogant Sicilian count that he was, his brown gaze cool and haughty as he looked at her, his facial features arrogantly remote.

Which should have made it easier for her to be around him.

But didn't.

That very remoteness, his detachment, made it

difficult for her to believe last night had happened at all—let alone know how to deal with it.

Stephen squeezed her hand. 'I want you to go home for a while, Angel,' he encouraged gruffly. 'I'm only going to take a nap, anyway, so you may as well take advantage of the opportunity to get something hot to eat, and at least take a shower and have a change of clothes.'

She eyed him teasingly. 'Is that a polite way of telling me I look a mess?'

'It's a polite way of telling you to go home and take a rest!' Stephen smiled. 'Neither of you can have got much sleep, staying here last night.'

Angelica couldn't even look at Wolf as she felt the warm colour enter her cheeks. She had no idea whether or not Wolf had slept last night or not, although the grimness of his expression seemed to imply not. *She* had slept long and deeply after Wolf had made love to her. In fact, she couldn't remember sleeping that well for a long, long time. If ever…

'Stephen's right, Angel,' Wolf put in evenly, his dark gaze easily holding hers as she looked at him sharply. 'It won't do anyone any good if you collapse from exhaustion and lack of food.'

He, better than anyone, Angelica knew, had to know that after last night she was completely rested!

'Please do this, Angel. For me,' Stephen encouraged firmly.

'Oh, very well,' she conceded, after another quick glance at Wolf's uncompromising expression and Stephen's equally determined one. 'But there really is no need for Wolf to accompany me,' she added deliberately.

Wolf's mouth twisted. 'I need a shower and change of clothes too; I slept in these last night.' He looked down at his crumpled shirt and creased denims.

The heat burned even hotter in Angelica's cheeks as she acknowledged that her own jeans were fine—testament to the fact that she *hadn't* slept in them last night!

'I'll go home to grab some food, and a shower and change of clothes, but after that I'm coming straight back,' Angelica warned Stephen as she moved to pick up her shoulder bag. 'I really don't need any more sleep.'

'Stubborn child,' Stephen murmured affectionately, as she bent down to kiss him warmly on the cheek. 'Thank you for being here, darling,' he said. 'It was knowing you would be that brought me back, you know.'

She did know. Just as she knew that one day she would tell him that her mother had been here too yesterday. If nothing else, Stephen deserved to know that Mrs Harper had been concerned enough—not just about Angelica, but about him too—to drive up to London, to stay until she knew he was out of danger. Who knew? Maybe one day Stephen, her mother and Neil might even become friends. Stranger things had happened.

Such as Wolf Gambrelli making love to her…!

She tried to put all thoughts of that from her mind as Wolf took a firm hold of her arm and they left Stephen's room together. The two of them walked along the corridor in silence as they made their way to the exit, that silence not in the least comfortable, but filled with expectant tension.

Angelica drew in a ragged breath after several minutes of almost being dragged along in Wolf's wake as she tried to match her stride to his forceful one, knowing that even if she did manage to put all thoughts of last night out of her head—which she doubted!—Wolf obviously couldn't. 'Wolf—'

'Not now, Angel,' he rasped hardly, without so much as a glance in her direction.

His jaw was clenched, a pulse beating there, and his expression was becoming even more remote.

She sighed. 'I only wanted to say that I think it best if we both forget what happened last night.'

Forget it? Wolf echoed hollowly to himself.

How the hell could he forget it when just touching her arm like this, once again feeling the soft silk of her skin against his fingers, filled his head with erotic memories of how silky, how sensitive, responsive, other parts of her body were?

'Consider it forgotten,' he bit back, determinedly keeping his gaze straight ahead, knowing that to look at her would be his undoing, that at this moment he wanted nothing more than to take her back to bed and finish what they had started. His unsated body ached with desire!

She gave him a sharp glance. 'Just like that…?'

He nodded tersely. 'Just like that.'

Wolf could tell by the sudden rigidity of her arm beneath his fingers, her tension, that she was either hurt or angry at his dismissal. But he had no intention of even attempting to find out which emotion it was.

This woman had somehow got under his skin in a way that had never happened to him before, had pierced the armour he usually wore about his emotions, and he didn't like the feeling!

He didn't like it at all.

He had known Angel only a matter of days, and for most of that time he hadn't trusted her sudden advent into Stephen's life.

But yesterday, in her absolute relief that

Stephen had survived his operation, Wolf had seen beyond a shadow of a doubt that Angel's feelings for Stephen were genuine—as were those of her mother. His own suspicions about Angel's motives for being in Stephen's life, and those of her family, were completely unfounded.

Leaving Wolf with no idea how he now felt about Angel.

And a part of him—the self-preserving part of him, the part of him that had always distanced him from personal involvement, that wanted no part of the Gambrelli Curse—didn't want to know, either.

A few more days—a week at the most—and Stephen would be out of hospital. Then Wolf could excuse himself and leave. This week couldn't pass quickly enough as far as he was concerned!

An hour later, Angelica studied her naked reflection in the floor-to-ceiling mirror in her bedroom, after returning from taking her shower in the *en suite* bathroom, her head tilted to one side as she tried to detect if she looked any different from when she had left Stephen's home yesterday.

It had been a mere twenty-four hours.

But it had been twenty-four hours in which Angelica knew she had certainly come to *feel* different.

She had never reached the ultimate in physical pleasure before—had never known such intimacy with anyone, never allowed the liberties that Wolf had taken as if they'd been his by right.

Her body had definitely felt different as she'd soaped herself beneath the hot shower spray—much more sensitised, as if it was already expectantly aroused in anticipation of a lover. In anticipation of Wolf...

She considered the curves of her body in the mirror: her pert breasts, the hollow slope of her stomach, the gentle curve of her hips, the apex between her thighs.

No, she finally decided. Apart from a certain deepened rosiness to the tips of her breasts, there was no visible physical evidence of the effect of Wolf's ministrations the night before.

But her body felt different. Her breasts felt heavy, their nipples engorged and sensitive, and the continuing and unaccustomed ache between her thighs was equally unnerving.

And that was just at the *memory* of Wolf's lovemaking the night before!

What—?

She turned sharply to the door as she heard a knock. 'Just a minute,' she urged, slightly impatiently, and she moved to collect her robe—coming to a halt halfway across the bedroom, her eyes widening with shock as Wolf entered the room.

Wolf stopped in the doorway, feeling as if all the breath had been knocked from his body as he found himself staring at a completely naked Angel.

It had been semi-dark the night before when he'd kissed and caressed her luscious curves. Only the touch of his hands and lips had told him how utterly desirable Angel was. But now she was standing completely naked in the middle of her bedroom, like a fawn caught in the headlights of a car, he was finally able to see just how beautiful she really was.

So beautiful she left him speechless!

Her hair was a wild dark tangle about the slenderness of her shoulders, her breasts were firm and uptilted, the rosy tips pouting invitingly; her waist and hips undulated gently, while dark curls sat at the apex of her thighs, above long and shapely legs.

And, he realised, he was staring at all that ripe, inviting nakedness like a starving man contemplating a feast!

He stiffened. 'I thought you told me to come in…' he said tautly.

Her mouth quirked. 'Obviously not.' She sighed wearily as she reached for the grey silk robe which lay on the bed. 'Although this is nothing that you haven't seen before, is it?' she remarked as she slid her arms into the robe, her fingers shaking slightly as she belted it tightly about the slenderness of her waist before looking across at him challengingly. 'What can I do for you, Wolf?' she prompted.

Wolf was pretty sure, from the rise of her dark brows, that she didn't really want him to answer that truthfully.

Although the unmistakable hard stirring of his body probably answered her without the need for words!

He stepped inside the bedroom—a bedroom that was clearly put by for Angel's use when she stayed here with Stephen, if the amount of her personal things about the room was anything to go by—closing the door behind him, not sure of the sensibility of doing that, but unwilling to run the risk of any of Stephen's household staff being witness to their conversation.

His mouth went dry as he watched Angel reach up and untangle her hair from the collar of her robe, the silky material stretching tautly across her breasts as she did so, clearly outlining her hardened nipples to his captivated gaze.

This was ridiculous, Wolf told himself firmly. He had seen dozens of naked women in his thirty-six years—made love to quite a number of them too. But never before had he been aroused just at the sight of a woman's naked body.

It had to be the memory of touching those beguiling curves the night before, of kissing them, tasting them, that made his thighs ache and roused his senses to full alert!

Angelica regarded Wolf's distracted expression, feeling more than a little embarrassed at having him walk in on her in this way, but determined not to react like a gauche schoolgirl and so let Wolf know how much his seeing her naked disturbed her. Better that he continue to believe she was nothing but a little gold-digger than—

'I am here because, after yesterday, I realise that I owe you an apology,' he confessed flatly.

Colour warmed her cheeks. 'I thought we had agreed to forget about last night—'

'I am referring to your feelings for Stephen, not what happened between the two of us last night,' Wolf cut in impatiently. 'I have realised, after seeing your obvious relief at the success of Stephen's operation, that I may have—misjudged your intentions towards him.'

So Wolf *didn't* still believe she was a gold-digger…?

'May have?' she echoed dryly.

His jaw tightened. 'I *have* misjudged your

feelings for him,' he corrected tautly, his hands clenched at his sides.

Angelica gave a derisive inclination of her head. 'You most certainly have,' she confirmed; after the things he had accused her of, she felt totally unsympathetic to his obvious embarrassment at having to make the admission.

'Those of your family too,' Wolf added uncomfortably. 'Your mother was obviously genuinely concerned when she came to the clinic yesterday. And not just on your account.'

My, my, my, he *was* suffering a guilt-trip, wasn't he? Angelica acknowledged.

And not before time!

The embarrassment she had warned him about at the weekend, that he would feel once he knew who she really was, was a little later in coming than she had expected. But it had come, and Wolf was clearly disconcerted at having to admit he had been wrong about her.

He obviously wasn't a man who liked to be proved wrong!

She moved to sit on the side of the bed, crossing her legs at the knees as she looked across at him expectantly, the silky material of her robe falling back to reveal the length of her legs.

Wolf willed himself not to look at their expanse,

or to allow himself to dwell on thoughts of her nakedness beneath her robe, keeping his gaze firmly on her face, his thoughts guarded.

'Well?' she finally prompted.

He gave a self-derisive shake of his head. 'Of course you wish me to leave—'

'What I wish is for you to apologise, Wolf!' Angel corrected him impatiently. 'Admitting you were wrong isn't quite the same as an actual apology, now, is it?'

She really wanted her pound of flesh, Wolf thought frustratedly. And why shouldn't she? He had already admitted to himself last night that because of his suspicions about her he had been unnecessarily cruel to her over the weekend— said things, made accusations that now made him cringe to remember them. An actual apology was definitely in order.

He drew in a ragged breath. 'I am sorry for the insulting remarks I made to you over the weekend,' he conceded. 'Stephen was right about you and I was wrong,' he added. 'What more do you want me to say, Angel?' he exclaimed, as she continued to look at him expectantly.

She gave him a mysterious smile. 'Nothing,' she assured him. 'I was just—savouring the moment,' she explained.

Wolf's hands clenched and unclenched at his sides as he resisted the impulse to cross the room and pull her up into his arms.

The little devil was enjoying his discomfort and openly laughing at him!

His jaw clenched as he fought an inward battle to avoid taking her in his arms, crushing his mouth down onto hers to wipe that laughter from her lips and force her into a physical acknowledgement of him.

After lying awake for hours the night before, fantasising about making complete love to this woman, about burying himself to the hilt in her ready softness, he knew that to even touch her now would be a mistake on his part, that his self-control would shatter into a million pieces.

That *wasn't* going to happen!

He pulled himself together. 'I will leave you to finish dressing.'

'How kind of you,' she came back archly.

Wolf held on to his temper with effort. 'I believe the cook has prepared a brunch for us.'

'I asked her to,' Angel confirmed lightly.

There really was nothing else to say, Wolf acknowledged. He had made the apology he had come here to make, and now he needed to get out of Angel's bedroom.

Except that his legs were refusing to obey his instruction for them to move!

'Was there something else, Wolf…?' Angelica asked guardedly as he made no effort to leave.

'*No*! No,' he repeated, less aggressively. 'Nothing else.'

Then why didn't he leave?

'I have no intention of telling Stephen what happened between the two of us last night, if that's what bothering you,' she assured him, her cheeks burning hotly just remembering the way she had given herself to this man the night before.

Wolf's nostrils flared, his cheeks and jaw hard, his mouth a thin line, and his brown eyes glittering determinedly. 'I give you my assurance that such a thing will not happen again.'

Angelica frowned, not so sure she could make such a promise herself.

Even now she was completely aware of the lines of his muscled body beneath the white polo shirt and tailored black trousers he had changed into, of the slight dampness to his burnished gold hair following his own shower, of the long sensitivity of his hands—hands that had touched her so intimately the night before…

Her gaze returned to his face, captured by the firm sensuality of his mouth, the lips that had kissed her, known her, driven her to a release that still made her body ache with remembered pleasure.

But this was Wolf Gambrelli, she reminded herself, Womaniser extraordinaire. Of *course* she had reached orgasm in his arms—because he had known exactly which buttons to press in order to facilitate her release; the man probably knew his way around a woman's body better than she did!

Her spine straightened determinedly. 'I'm pleased to hear it,' she replied caustically.

Wolf's brows rose. 'Are you?'

'Yes,' she assured him firmly. 'Now, if you wouldn't mind, I really would like to get back to the hospital as soon as possible.'

His lips thinned humourlessly as he nodded. 'Of course. I will see you downstairs shortly,' he told her, before turning and leaving her bedroom.

Angelica stared after him, very aware that Wolf's apology had been a hollow victory—that, despite everything, he'd had the last word.

And that last word had been to assure her that he had no intention of making love to her again.

To her confusion, she wasn't sure whether his assurance made her feel relieved or disappointed…

CHAPTER TEN

STEPHEN'S recovery, during the week following his operation, had been miraculous as far as Angelica was concerned.

The time she necessarily had had to spend in Wolf's company had gone less quickly; the two of them had been so polite to each other whenever they were around Stephen that it had almost made her wince, but the times when they'd found themselves alone—being driven to and from the clinic, usually—had been spent in silence. And Wolf had chosen to spend his evenings in Stephen's study—presumably dealing with the paperwork connected with his own and Stephen's business interests.

But Wolf had kept to his promise to act as her protector—had undoubtedly been useful in fending off the intrusive questions of the reporters who had appeared outside the clinic the day following Stephen's operation.

Although it had been a little embarrassing to

find her name linked with Wolf's rather than Stephen's in the newspapers the following morning—the general consensus seemed to be that she was Wolf's latest girlfriend!

But Wolf hadn't seemed concerned about that misconception, and Stephen had found it highly amusing when he'd seen the photographs and conjecture over the two of them being together. So Angelica had decided not to make a fuss over it, either.

After all, she decided as she glanced from beneath long lashes across the dinner table at Wolf, on the evening prior to Stephen's discharge from the clinic, Count Gambrelli would be leaving her life for good in the next couple of days, which would completely blow away that particular misconception.

It was probably time—past time—that she and Stephen acknowledged their true connection, anyway.

In the meantime, having visited Stephen at the clinic earlier, she only had dinner this evening with Wolf to get through, and then tomorrow they would be bringing Stephen home.

'I want to thank you for all your help this last week, Wolf,' she told him, knowing she owed him that at least.

Angel was dismissing him, Wolf knew, and he found himself filled with an irritated impatience at the realisation.

Which was ridiculous, when he had been doing everything he could this last week to avoid being alone in her company, determined there would be no repeat of that night at the clinic. The attraction he felt towards Angel was endangering everything he held dear. Namely, his decision never to succumb to the Gambrelli Curse!

But the fact that she had been avoiding him in exactly the same way rankled slightly!

He wasn't a conceited man—at least, he had never thought of himself as such—but he had to admit he had found Angel's assured aloofness this last week grating on his already frayed self-control.

It hadn't helped that, in sharp contrast to her coolness, he had found himself constantly aware of everything she did and said!

Like now.

She looked fantastic this evening—the gunmetal-grey dress she wore a perfect match for her misty-coloured eyes, its simplicity of style emphasising the fullness of her breasts, leaving her arms bare as well as her legs below its knee-length. Her hair fell in a silky dark cloud about her shoulders and down her spine, and her make-up was light—just a peach gloss on the tempting pout of her lips.

They hadn't been in the habit of dining together like this. Wolf usually managing to have his evening meal on a tray in the study. But, with Stephen's discharge imminent, the older man had decided to look over his own paperwork this evening at the clinic, giving Wolf no excuse not to dine with Angel once they returned from visiting.

But perhaps, in the interest of self-defence, he should have found one!

'I was only too pleased to be of assistance,' he replied coolly to her thanks.

Her eyes gleamed mischievously. 'Were you?'

Wolf frowned slightly as he saw that gleam; obviously he wasn't the only one who felt a certain relief that the strain of the two of them living alone here together this last week was about to end. But no doubt for different reasons...

Although her relief wasn't exactly flattering to a man's ego, he acknowledged self-derisively.

Not that he'd ever expected flattery from Angel; she was honest to the point of bluntness. Especially where her opinion of him and the numerous women he'd had in his life was concerned.

'Of course,' he confirmed tersely.

Angelica eyed him drolly. 'You're being very

polite, Wolf,' she observed. 'When really you must be longing to get back to your own life?' she added questioningly, aware that he had put his own interests on hold this last week, as he kept his promise to Stephen to stay at the house and protect her.

He hadn't gone out even one evening to meet friends or family of his own. Angelica had been completely aware of his presence in the house when they weren't visiting Stephen, even if the two of them hadn't spent any of that time together.

But no doubt there was a woman somewhere, waiting impatiently for Wolf to return to her bed...

'I'm sure this week has been a great trial for you,' she said, before he could answer.

'Not at all,' he dismissed, hooded lids low over those piercing dark eyes as he sat back in his chair to look across the table at her. 'It has allowed us to spend time together.'

And that was a good thing?

Somehow Angelica couldn't see Wolf thinking of it in that way.

Besides which, Wolf had kept himself so aloof this last week that he hadn't allowed her to get to know him any better at all!

She had already known that Wolf was a good friend to Stephen—even the initial wrong assumptions he had made about her had been born out of concern for his friend. Just as she had already been aware that Wolf valued his family.

Even more disturbing, she had already known that he was devastatingly attractive to women.

To *her!*

It was impossible for her to deny that, after her response to him a week ago, just thinking about it was still enough to make her tremble with awareness.

Especially when he looked as elegantly handsome as he did tonight, in a dark tailored suit and snowy white shirt, a pale grey tie knotted meticulously at his throat, his over-long blond hair curling silkily on the broadness of his shoulders.

Maybe she had discovered something else, after all…

Much as she wished it weren't so.

Much as she wanted to deny it.

She was more attracted to Wolf now than she had been even a week ago!

From the way her blood pounded through her veins just at the sight of him, the way her heart leapt in her chest, her nerve-endings tingling, a rush of heat coursing through her body whenever she was near him, there was a distinct possibility that what she now felt towards him was more than just attraction…

Towards a man who discarded women from his life with the same casualness with which other men discarded disposable razorblades? she attempted to remind herself.

But, attracted or not, Angelica just did not intend becoming another notch on Wolf Gambrelli's bedpost. Which meant that any deeper emotions she may or may not feel towards him had to be suppressed...

'Oh, dear,' she came back mockingly. 'Poor you.'

'Not at all,' Wolf came back softly, his gaze narrowed on the beauty of her face, knowing from her deliberately teasing expression as she defiantly met his eyes that she had no intention of letting him read her thoughts.

He couldn't help wondering why...

'Angel—what is it?' he questioned harshly. She had backed sharply away from him when he reached out to touch her hand with his, where it rested on the tabletop.

'Nothing.' She turned away, fussing with placing her napkin more precisely across her thighs.

'It is...something,' Wolf insisted slowly, looking at the paleness of her face. 'Angel—'

'Will you please stop calling me that?' she implored.

Wolf regarded her consideringly: her eyes had

taken on a haunted look now, two bright spots of colour in her cheeks, her lips clamped tightly together, her chin set determinedly, her breasts quickly rising and falling as she breathed agitatedly.

Breasts that were clearly outlined against the soft material of her dress, the nipples familiarly and tellingly hard…

His gaze returned to that delicate blush on her cheeks.

Maybe Angel *hadn't* been feeling as aloofly assured this last week as she had wanted him to believe…?

Maybe, just maybe, she had been fighting the same attraction he had?

'Why?' he taunted softly.

'I've told you why!' she exclaimed, anger snapping in those expressive grey eyes as she glared across at him. 'You don't have the right—'

'I beg to differ,' Wolf drawled, his gaze once again roaming with slow deliberation over the slender curves of her body, pausing at that pointed thrust of her breasts before moving sharply back to meet her own briefly unguarded gaze.

What he saw there made his breath catch in his throat. Angel Harper was as physically aware of him as he was of her, and she wanted him so badly she was almost panting with that need!

He gave a hard smile. 'I believe you gave me that right the night you fell apart in my arms—'

'How dare you even mention that night?' she interrupted accusingly as she stood up. 'I was overwrought after Stephen's operation. An emotional wreck—'

'All this indignant anger on your part is nothing but a front, Angel,' Wolf pointed out, his confidence in his conclusions growing at her over-emotional outburst; a cool set-down would have been much more applicable to his challenge than all this fiery anger. 'To hide what you are really feeling.'

Her face crumpled slightly. 'And what would *you* know about what I'm feeling?' she challenged. 'What would *you* know about emotion at all when it's something that you avoid like the plague?'

'Some emotions, yes.' He gave an acknowledging inclination of his head. 'However, I do not believe I am the hypocrite that you are—'

'How dare you?' she cut in heatedly, hands clenched at her sides as her eyes shot sparks across the table at him.

'How dare I?' Wolf repeated consideringly. 'Let me see…' he murmured. 'Oh, yes,' he drawled, as if just coming to a realisation. 'I *dare*, Angel—' his voice hardened forcefully, dark eyes glittering as he sat forward '—because this last week you have been treating me like that plague victim you just mentioned—when all the time you have been so badly wanting me to repeat our lovemaking that you have ached with it!'

Angelica gasped. 'That's a lie—'

'Is it?' he responded. 'Would you like to put that claim to the test?' He threw his own napkin down and stood up.

Angelica eyed him warily, her breathing shallow. There was a dangerous tension between them. What did he—?

'No!' she gasped as she suddenly recognised the raw intent in his eyes. 'Absolutely not,' she warned firmly even as she began to back away from the table. From Wolf. 'I don't want this…I don't want *you*!' she insisted breathlessly.

'Little hypocrite,' he repeated scornfully, and he moved around the table to follow her.

Angelica didn't wait around to see what Wolf was going to do when he reached her.

She ran.

Out of the small dining room, across the wide reception area, up the wide staircase, along the gallery and down the hallway into her bedroom.

She only realised as she turned back to close the door that Wolf had dogged her every step. That he now stood just inside her bedroom doorway, the intent in his glittering gaze having intensified during the chase.

'You can't do this, Wolf,' she breathed desperately, shaking her head even as she began to back away from that intent.

Wolf moved into the room to close the door softly, carefully, behind him before turning back to face her. 'I am going to do nothing that we haven't both been wanting for the last week,' he told her, and he began to close the distance between them.

Angelica kept her widened gaze on him as she took several more steps backwards, briefly feeling the bed against the back of her knees before she overbalanced and fell back on the mattress.

'Yes…!' Wolf verbalised his satisfaction as he moved over her, a hand on either side of her head as he looked down at her, his thighs pressing intimately against hers.

Thighs that were already hardened with desire, Angelica recognised achingly, even as she felt an answering rush of warmth between her own thighs as he fitted that hardness snugly against her.

Wolf was right, she acknowledged weakly; she *did* want him. She had spent the last week wanting him. She wanted him so badly now that she was going to shatter with disappointment if he didn't soon take her.

If she didn't soon take *him!*

Her arms moved up across the muscled width of his shoulders to encircle his nape. Grey eyes locked with chocolate-brown as she pulled him towards her.

Wolf gave a groan as he allowed Angel to pull him down, already so aroused he was rigid with need.

His mouth captured hers, and he took his weight on his elbows, moving his hands to cup each side of her face and hold her beneath him as his lips and tongue ravaged her softness.

She was hot, so hot—her skin burning, the tips of her breasts, naked beneath her dress, hot and hard against the thin material. But even that item of clothing was too much between him and her silken nakedness.

Wolf took Angel with him as he rolled onto his back. Now Angel was the one who lay on top, her kiss as fevered as his as one of his hands moved to slowly slide the zip of her dress down the slender length of her spine.

Slowly because he wanted to enjoy, to savour every single moment of this possession. He had every intention of making Angel groan and squirm above him as sweet pleasure engulfed her, engulfed both of them.

Her lips, swollen and needy, stayed with his

even as she slid her arms from the dress, their tongues duelling, their breathing rapid and ragged in the silence of the room.

He had been wrong: she wasn't completely naked beneath her dress. She was wearing a thin satin camisole, and her breasts felt glorious as his hands moved to cup her, full and heavy above him, the soft pad of his thumbs instinctively finding the burning tips as he stroked them.

With a gasp Angel broke their kiss, her hands clinging to his shoulders as her back arched, her head was thrown back.

Wolf's gaze was upon her face now as he pleasured the ripe swell of her breasts. His movements were urgent as he slid the thin straps of her camisole over her arms, tugging them down, releasing her breasts to his hungry gaze, full and engorged. He cupped her as he drew her into his mouth and began to feast.

Tasting, licking, suckling, he took the peak deeper into the heat of his mouth and Angel achingly groaned his name, her thighs parting to the hardness of his erection, pointing against her soft mound. His hands moved beneath her dress to cup her bottom and hold her against him as his erection found her own arousal and he began to move slowly, rhythmically, against that heat.

Angelica breathed haltingly as sensation after sensation rocked her body. Wolf's mouth, lips and tongue were paying homage to her breasts even as his thighs moved against hers, rubbing against her through the silk of her panties. She could feel the rush of moisture between her thighs, knew she was swollen and open to him. That she wanted him inside her!

Now.

Urgently.

Wolf, as if in answer to her whimpering pleas, rolled them both to the side, his mouth capturing hers as one of his hands moved assuredly to the wetness between her thighs, gently probing beneath the silk of her panties.

Angelica melted weakly against him as he searched for and found her hard, sensitised flesh and his fingers began to stroke, soft and then hard. Her hips arched instinctively into his arousing caress as she felt the pressure building within her, the heat intensifying with each touch of his fingers, knowing she was spiralling out of control even as she felt the waves of release begin to wash over and through her, deep, deep within her.

Wolf's mouth was against hers, his tongue thrusting deep into her mouth, as she reached a climax of indescribable pleasure, and his fingers continued to stroke her as it seemed her release would never end.

She lay back on the bed, breathless, boneless, awash in a sea of sensations where only Wolf and she existed. Her arms moved up about his shoulders as he once again moved over her, and she pulled him down into a kiss of such sweet pleasure that she felt as if she had died and gone to heaven.

A heaven where desire, wanting, need, were quickly re-aroused as Wolf quickly threw off his clothes and came back into her arms, wonderfully, magnificently naked. His body was satin skin over hard muscle and sinew, sleekly powerful, and the wildness of his blond hair gave him a recklessly piratical appearance as he looked down at her before gently nudging her thighs apart.

'Not yet,' she murmured silkily, aware that twice now Wolf had brought her to the peak of desire without once reaching that magical plane himself. Her need to have him inside her was put on hold as she turned to move up onto her knees and push him back down on the bed.

'I want you *now*,' Wolf groaned achingly, his eyes dark.

'Soon,' Angelica soothed throatily, and she moved to trail featherlight, open-mouthed kisses across the hard lines of his chest, the long length of her hair trailing tantalisingly across his sensitised flesh. Wolf tensed as she paused to explore the deep well of his navel, lips and tongue making a leisurely foray.

She was trying to drive him insane, Wolf decided breathlessly. His back arched, his hands tightly gripping the bedclothes as she continued her exploration, her mouth dewy as she trailed a path down to the pulsing hardness between his thighs.

Absolutely, thoroughly insane, he acknowledged, as he felt the heaven of her lips against him, of her tongue flicking out to trail moistly from base to tip of his hard shaft. Those lips were encircling the sensitised tip, sending shivers of pleasure convulsing through him even as she cupped him lower down, fingers lightly caressing even as her tongue travelled over and around him.

That tongue laved and tasted, while those hands continued their caress, first cupping him, then featherlight against his inner thigh. And all the time the heat of her mouth was driving him recklessly on.

'No more, Angel!' he finally urged, and his hands moved abruptly, fingers tightly gripping her wrists, as he pulled her away from him and up the length of his body until she was lying on top of him. His hands cupped each side of her face and he looked up at her hungrily. 'I want to be inside you. Deep inside you,' he added forcefully, and he rolled.

Angel was now lying once again beneath him, and his thighs were sliding in between hers as his hardness probed and entered her swollen entrance.

'Deep, deep, inside you,' he promised, and he surged into her heat, her wetness.

Angel took him, all of him, her muscles clamping tightly around him as her body spasmed and then settled to his rhythm as he moved in and then slowly out of her.

It took every effort of Wolf's self-control to keep his movements slow and gentle, to allow her tightness to become accustomed to him, for her body to adapt to the size and hardness of him. His teeth were gritted, and sweat broke out on his brow as he stroked his hips slowly in and against her, nearly losing his grip on that control as he heard her gasps, her throaty cries, felt her hands tightly gripping his shoulders as she began to move urgently against him.

He gentled her urgency and slowed to roll his hips against hers, his thrusts more shallow, sliding, gliding against her inner sensitivity, his gaze capturing and holding hers as he brought her again and again to the edge of release, only to hold her there, to wait for those spasms to subside, before once again beginning those shallow thrusts. Gently, oh-so-gently, her inner softness convulsed and tightened about him.

Minutes later, as she wrapped her legs about his waist and pulled him surgingly deep inside her, he knew that she could wait no longer—that Angel's time had come.

Her eyes widened and her breathing was snatched as he sank himself fully inside her, like a sword in the snugness of its sheath. And Wolf was able to see as well as feel when, seconds later, she reached that second climax. Deep, intense satisfaction welled within him as he felt her muscles tighten and then swell around him, and he watched the way her face filled with the sheer pleasure of her release, eyes closed, cheeks flushed, her lips slightly parted as she lay back, limp and replete upon the bed.

'Look at me, Angel,' he encouraged gently, one hand moving up to cup the delicacy of her face. 'I want you to look at me as I looked at you,' he pressed huskily.

Angelica raised heavy lids, her eyes dark as she looked up into his face. Those hard, unrelenting planes were softened with desire, want and need. There was a flush to his cheeks, and his eyes burned darkly before he bent his head and closed his mouth over her capturing the hard tip of her breast. Once again, his thighs began to move over and in her, and her hands caressed the hard contours of his back, his shoulders, tightly gripping the hair at his nape as their bodies moved together in primitive rapture.

Unbelievably, minutes later, she felt Wolf surrender to his own release; he seemed to grow inside her, to swell as if he completely filled her. His neck arched, his eyes closed, his control completely gone as he took Angelica with him into that vortex where heat and fire burned them, fused them into one.

CHAPTER ELEVEN

WOLF opened his eyes to darkness, realising as he did so that he must have slept. That they must both have slept, he acknowledged, with a slight catch in his throat as he heard the steady rhythm of Angel's breathing beside him in the darkness.

In her bed.

Where he had followed her.

Where the two of them had made love—an experience more complete, more compelling, than anything Wolf had ever experienced in his life before.

Never before had he shared such fierceness followed by such gentleness, and then again that fierceness—taking quickly following giving, as they both surrendered to the freedom of the senses, to the pleasure they found together beyond words, beyond reasoning.

Beyond what Wolf wanted to reason.

He glanced at the woman who lay sleeping

beside him, her head resting on his shoulder, one of her hands splayed across his chest. Her hair was a dark shadow on the whiteness of the pillow behind her, her face all shadows as his gaze adjusted to the silvery light of the moon shining in through a window.

What had this woman done to him?

What was it about her alone that made him want to linger here beside her? To wait for her to wake up and then make love to her again, to hold her captive here as once again he drove them both to that edge of madness?

Edge of madness?

They had gone over that edge and beyond, far beyond, to a plain, a plateau, where Wolf had never been before with any woman.

And that scared the hell out of him!

He moved slightly, sliding his arm out from under Angel, untangling his limbs from hers as he edged to the side of the bed and sat up, briefly burying his face in his hands before standing decisively to begin pulling on his clothes.

Angelica knew—sensed—the moment Wolf's warmth left her. Lifting heavy lids, allowing a few moments for her eyes to get used to the gloom, she gently turned and saw him standing across the room, almost fully dressed, his back towards her as he buttoned up his shirt.

She would have spoken then—sleepily, invitingly—but as he turned she saw his face: his expression was grim, his lips tight and set, his jaw clenched and his eyes glitteringly hard in the moonlight.

Not the face of an indulgent and eager lover, but the face of a man who just wanted to get away from here—from her!

Her words were caught and held in her throat. A throat that burned with unshed tears as she realised that last night had meant something completely different to Wolf than it had to her.

For her it had been a realisation, a revelation. She knew that she had fallen in love with him. Deeply, irrevocably.

For Wolf it had obviously been nothing more than another conquest, no doubt made all the sweeter for him because it had been *her,* a woman who had made no secret of her scorn for the way he lived.

No doubt…?

It would definitely have been sweet—because he had won her arousal, her complete capitulation; those things would have made him all the more triumphant because of her previous attitude.

She continued to watch him—beneath lowered

lids, knowing that if he should glance her way he would assume she was still asleep.

He didn't look at her. Not once.

Instead he bent down to grab his jacket from the floor, before moving purposefully, stealthily, towards the door, careful not to wake her as he quietly let himself out of the room.

Angelica's breath caught on a sob as the door slowly clicked closed behind him.

She loved Wolf!

She had absolutely no doubt, knew there was no room for manouevre. She loved Wolf—had given herself to him as well as taking from him. Oh, he had given and taken too. But not for the same reason.

Wolf didn't love her.

Wolf would never love her.

She turned over in the bed, a ball of misery beneath the bedclothes as she allowed the hot tears to fall…

Wolf glanced at Angel from beneath half-lowered lids as they sat in the back of the chauffeur-driven car on their way to the clinic to bring Stephen home.

Angel was pale and composed as she sat beside him, looking coolly beautiful in a cream blouse and black fitted trousers, her hair—that long, glorious hair that Wolf had buried his face in the night before—confined in a black velvet bow at her neck.

She hadn't joined him in the breakfast room earlier. His first glimpse of her had been when she had come down the stairs to join him in the hallway before the two of them walked out to the car.

The silence between them now stretched like a taut piece of string in danger of snapping; for once, Wolf was not at all sure of what to do or say next.

Thank you for last night. I enjoyed it.

You're the best I've ever known.

Maybe we can do it again some time—like in a thousand years or so!

There was nothing he could think of to say that didn't seem to add insult to injury.

And he *had* injured Angel. He knew that he had been the one to instigate what had happened last night, that Angel had told him no before he'd decided to persuade her otherwise, before he had seduced her into deciding otherwise.

Damn it, this silence between them was intolerable!

Angel was twenty-six years old, and he hadn't been her first lover any more than she had been his, so what was the problem?

There wasn't one, he dismissed impatiently. They were both consenting adults, and he would have stopped at any time in their lovemaking last night if Angel really had been reluctant. The truth of the matter was she hadn't been. She *so* hadn't been!

Then why did he feel this damned uncomfortable?

The two of them would have to break this air of tension between them before they reached the clinic, Angelica recognised heavily. Before they reached Stephen. Before Stephen, who was one of the most astute men she had ever known, realised that something had gone seriously wrong between his daughter and the man he considered his closest friend since he'd seen them together yesterday evening.

Her tongue moved nervously across the stiffness of her lips before she spoke. 'The traffic doesn't seem too heavy this morning,' she commented lightly as she glanced out of the window beside her.

'No,' Wolf replied tersely.

'We should make good time.'

'Yes.'

'Let's hope there aren't too many reporters waiting outside this morning.'

'Yes.'

'Perhaps—'

'For God's sake, Angel, you'll be discussing the

weather next!' Wolf bit out as he turned on the leather seat to face her. 'What we should really be talking about is last night—'

'No. It isn't,' Angelica cut in firmly, at the same time giving a significant glance at the chauffeur; the man might be discreet, but he certainly wasn't deaf!

Wolf's brown eyes glittered briefly, angrily, before he sat forward and murmured something to the driver.

Angelica swallowed hard as the glass partition slowly rolled into place, separating the two of them in the back of the limousine from the chauffeur in front, behind the wheel. Not what Angelica had wanted at all. The very air seemed to crackle between her and Wolf.

'That was completely unnecessary,' she told Wolf a little disingenuously. 'I have nothing to say to you that I wouldn't want Derek to hear.'

'Perhaps I have something I want to say to you?' he came back swiftly.

Her mouth tightened. She was sure after the way Wolf had left her bed in the early hours— after the way he had *crept* out of her bed—that whatever he had to say to her wasn't something she wanted to hear.

She turned to him, a deliberately cheerful smile on her lips. 'Is it a regular practice of yours to indulge in post-mortems with your lovers the morning after?' Having had only one previous lover herself—a fumbling, inexperienced affair while she was at university that had lasted one night and never been repeated—she certainly felt no such inclination! 'Perhaps you want me to give you a rating out of ten?' Even in her inexperience she knew that Wolf, for her, had been a twelve! 'Or perhaps you want to take this opportunity to assure me it will never happen again?' She unashamedly reminded Wolf of his claim of a week ago.

Wolf drew in a sharp breath. 'It won't,' he told her flatly.

She gave a derisive laugh. 'I believe you've said that before!'

This time Wolf knew he meant it. He couldn't allow last night to happen again and still hold on to his sanity. His freedom!

His mouth thinned. 'There will be no repeat of last night for the simple reason that I am leaving this afternoon.'

He had made the decision when he'd returned to his own bedroom at two o'clock this morning. Sleep had completely eluded him and he'd paced the room instead, forcing the sensual memories of Angel from his head as he coldly, clinically, made his plans to leave.

Stephen was well past any danger now, and would be returning to his home this morning. Surely he would understand—readily accept?—that Wolf had his own business affairs that must be seen to after his week of absence?

And Angel, he had reasoned, would be overjoyed to see him go.

'That was a rather sudden decision, wasn't it?' Angelica observed, while inside her thoughts were racing.

Wolf was *leaving?*

This afternoon?

In just a few hours' time?

She didn't need him to add that she would never see him again—that in future he would ensure that his visits to Stephen never coincide with her own. It was all there in the harsh aloofness of his expression, making his mouth a thin, uncompromising line.

Wolf would make sure that he never saw her again…

'Not particularly.' He gave a dismissive shrug. 'I have fulfilled my obligation to Stephen, and now it is time for me to return to my own life.'

To return to that woman Angelica was sure was waiting for him somewhere—either here in London, or in some other major city in the world.

Now that his obligation had been fulfilled…

She swallowed hard, clearing the threat of tears from her throat, although the hard lump that had lodged in her chest still seemed as suffocating. 'I'm sure that will be best for all of us,' she agreed off-handedly.

'Yes,' Wolf replied tersely. 'I trust you will let me know if there are any repercussions from last night—'

'There won't be,' Angelica cut in quickly, her face having paled slightly at the iciness of Wolf's tone as he spoke of the possibility of her becoming pregnant from their night together.

His mouth tightened. 'Of course not,' he agreed. 'Then there is nothing more to be said.' He turned to look out of the window beside him.

Angelica continued to look at him for several long, painful seconds, before she turned sharply away to stare sightlessly out of the window on her side of the limousine.

This was awful. Worse than awful. After the way he had left her bedroom early this morning she certainly hadn't expected Wolf to behave like a sexually-enthralled lover when they met again, but neither had she thought that he would tell her he was leaving in a matter of hours.

Had she really been so awful in bed?

She had been inexperienced, she knew, and not at all what Wolf was used to. But surely her responses, her enthusiasm—oh, God!—should have made up for some of that inexperience? Obviously not enough to keep the interest of a man like Wolf...

How on earth were they to get through even the few hours they had left to spend together? Especially under Stephen's watchful eye?

Thankfully, it was Stephen's presence that made the next couple of hours bearable. His pleasure in being home again, in being back at the centre of his own world, more than made up for any lack of communication between Angelica and Wolf.

And there really *was* no communication. The two of them didn't speak to each other again after that conversation in the car. Both of them spoke to Stephen, but never to each other.

'Okay, would either of you care to tell me what's wrong?' Stephen asked, settling himself on the sofa in the drawing room after lunch prior to taking a nap, sizing up the two of them with shrewd blue eyes.

Angelica glanced quickly at Wolf before looking sharply away again, not at all reassured by the harsh aloofness in his expression—an expression that was becoming annoyingly familiar. 'Wrong?' she echoed lightly as she plumped the cushions behind Stephen's back.

'Wrong,' Stephen repeated determinedly, giving her a reproving look from beneath lowered brows before glancing across to where Wolf stood in front of the window.

Looking every inch a Sicilian god, Angelica acknowledged painfully. Wolf's hair gleamed golden in the sunshine that blazed in through the window behind him, and his shoulders were wide, his stomach muscled, in the pale lemon polo shirt he wore, with jeans that rested low on his hips and emphasised the lean length of his legs.

It didn't help that Angelica knew exactly what he looked like without those trappings of civilisation!

She shook her head. 'I have no idea what—'

'I believe the—reserve you may have sensed in Angelica today, and my own—distraction,' Wolf explained carefully, 'are due to the fact that Angelica is aware of my decision to leave later this afternoon. She knows I am searching for the right way to tell you of that decision.'

He had called her Angelica, she noted dully as she went to move over and stand beside the unlit fireplace, her expression guarded.

Wolf, after all the times she had told him not to use the more familiar shortened version of her name, had decided that now was the time to revert to formality between them.

Because the chase was over. Because last night she had succumbed to that fatal Gambrelli charm. Now there was no need for him to constantly try and unnerve her.

'And why would you find it so difficult to tell me of that decision, Wolf?' Stephen showed his confusion at that explanation. 'I don't have a problem with that. I am more than grateful for the time you've already given us.'

Wolf knew his explanation for Angel's obvious strain and his own distant behaviour was more than a little lame, but it had been the best he could come up with in the face of Stephen's direct challenge and Angel's obvious lack of an answer.

Wolf was very aware that as the morning had progressed the strain between himself and Angel had become more than intolerable—it had become impossible! So much so that obviously neither of them had managed to hide it from Stephen...

'I was more than happy to be of help,' he assured the older man. 'But Cesare and I are looking into a business venture together that I really need to turn my attention to.'

Stephen looked at him shrewdly. 'Anything I can get involved in?'

Considering there *was* no business venture with Cesare, that might prove a little difficult!

'Not at this point, no,' Wolf assured his friend. 'But I'll keep you informed.'

'Pity,' Stephen said. 'Well, I appreciate that you have things of your own that need your attention, but Angel and I will be sorry to see you leave,' he added warmly.

Wolf glanced across at Angel, sure that she would be as sorry to see him leave as she would be a toothache!

The blandness of her expression, the frostiness in her eyes as she easily returned his gaze, seemed to confirm that impression!

Now, having looked at her fully—the first time he had done so directly for some hours—Wolf didn't seem able to look away again. He noticed how her cream blouse was fashioned out of a sheer material that moved tantalisingly over the lacy bra she wore beneath it, flooding his mind, his senses, with visions of how she had looked above him last night, without any of that clothing, as she rode him to mindless pleasure.

He wanted her again!

Now.

Immediately.

Wanted to pick her up in his arms, carry her

upstairs to his bed, rip all the clothes from her body and his. Wanted to surge up into her hot, tight sheath and have her pleasure him again!

He wanted that so badly he burned with it, and his gaze was hot as he couldn't stop looking at her, his hands shaking before he clenched them into fists at his sides and clamped his jaw together so tightly it ached.

'You know—' Stephen broke off whatever he had been about to say to turn in the direction of the butler as he hovered in the doorway. 'Yes, Holmes?' he prompted.

'Mr and Mrs Gambrelli have called in the hope that they might see you, sir,' the elderly man informed him evenly.

Cesare? Cesare and Robin were here to see Stephen?

It was the last thing Wolf had expected when, minutes ago, he had invented a business venture with his cousin in order to facilitate his own quick departure!

A fabrication that Cesare could blow completely out of the water with one innocently puzzled raise of his expressive eyebrows…!

CHAPTER TWELVE

ANGELICA knew from photographs she had seen of him in the newspapers that Cesare Gambrelli was tall and dark-haired, swarthy skinned, with eyes as dark as Wolf's. But what she wasn't prepared for was the facial and physical likeness of the two men: the two of them could have been brothers rather than cousins.

The little boy that Cesare carried confidently, possibly a year or so old, had the same dark colouring. The likeness between the three Gambrelli males was unmistakable.

The woman who entered at Cesare's side, a baby cradled in her arms, was obviously Robin Gambrelli: a tall woman, very beautiful, with hair the colour of warm honey and the most fascinating violet-coloured eyes Angelica had ever seen. Her figure was incredibly slender, considering she had only given birth to her baby just over a week ago, and the warmth of her smile as she crossed the room to greet Stephen only added to her already stunning beauty.

'Wolf,' Cesare hailed his cousin as they shook hands. 'Your godson obviously wishes you to take him,' he added indulgently, as the little boy reached out his arms towards Wolf. 'I had not realised you would be here today?' Cesare raised a dark, questioning brow, his English more accented than his cousin's.

Seeing the two men standing together like this, the similarities were breathtaking; both were over six feet tall and lethally attractive, with those dark eyes and aristocratically patrician features.

In fact, Angelica wasn't sure that two adult Gambrelli males in the same room together wasn't more than a little overwhelming!

'Cesare, Robin,' Stephen greeted them, reaching a hand out to Angelica as he beckoned her to his side. 'I would like to introduce you both to my daughter—Angelica,' he announced proudly, as he held Angelica's hand in his.

The two of them had discussed this amongst other things—including Angelica's mother's brief visit on the day of Stephen's operation—one evening when they were alone together at the clinic, and they had decided that once Stephen came home they would drop any further pretence and tell people exactly what their relationship was.

Angelica just hadn't expected that her first introduction would be to Wolf's cousin and his wife!

'I am very pleased to meet you, Miss Foxwood.' Cesare Gambrelli was the first to recover from the surprise announcement, moving to take her free hand, his smile warm as he bent briefly over it to deliver a kiss.

'It's Harper,' she corrected pleasantly, once he had released her hand. 'But please do call me Angelica,' she invited.

'Angelica.' Robin Gambrelli greeted her with the same warmth as her husband. 'I hope you'll excuse us all barging in like this?' she went on. 'We wanted to visit Stephen while he was in the clinic, but they wouldn't allow the children in too, and there was absolutely no way Marco would have allowed us to go and see his Uncle Stephen without him!'

Uncle Stephen, Angelica recognised ruefully.

She had been surprised at the amount of visitors who'd come to the clinic to see Stephen after his operation had became public knowledge, having had no idea how many friends he had, how many other people cared about him. And now, it seemed, Cesare and Robin Gambrelli's children called him Uncle Stephen...

For the first time Angelica realised just how she had restricted Stephen's social life this last year, by refusing to meet any of his friends or allowing him to acknowledge her as his daughter; she also realised that Wolf was only one of the people Stephen had deliberately kept at a distance whenever Angelica was staying with him.

If anything, it just made her love Stephen more for the sacrifices she now knew he had made on her behalf.

'As you can all see, I'm perfectly fine,' Stephen assured Robin brightly. 'More than fine,' he added, with a proud smile up at Angelica.

Everyone seemed to be smiling, Angelica noted. Everyone except Wolf…

Despite the charming little boy he now held in his arms—his godson—Wolf still looked as grim as ever…

Wolf spoke softly to baby Marco, even though his real attention was centred on Angel's conversation with his cousin and his wife.

That Cesare and Robin were surprised to learn Stephen had a daughter was obvious, but after their initial reaction they had handled the surprise with their usual grace and confidence.

Totally unlike his own reaction on learning Angel's real identity just over a week ago.

In fact, it would have been better for him if Angel *had* been Stephen's latest mistress!

He watched as Angelica turned to Robin and the baby she still held in her arms.

'May I?' she prompted gently, reaching out at Robin's nod and gingerly folding back the gossimer-thin shawl wrapped about the baby. 'She's adorable!' she breathed softly, obviously totally enchanted by the baby's perfect peaches-and-cream complexion; the tiny girl had a perfect rosebud of a mouth, an equally small nose, and pale lashes the same colour as the dusting of golden hair on her head.

Wolf gave a silent groan as he saw Angel's response to the newborn. Most women—Angel certainly!—seemed to find babies—even ones that weren't their own—totally fascinating.

'Can I hold her?' Angel ventured.

'But of course,' Robin easily agreed, before placing the wee bundle in Angel's waiting arms.

Wolf gave another pained groan, his eyes darkening as he couldn't look away from Angel holding the baby. How right she looked with a baby in her arms…

'Did you say something, Wolf?' Cesare murmured mockingly as he stood at Wolf's side, one dark brow raised in retaliation as Wolf gave him a freezing glance.

'No, nothing,' Wolf grated, his jaw rigid as he turned away from the speculation he could clearly see in Cesare's mildly amused gaze.

'Sorry, I thought you did.' The mockery in his cousin's voice had only deepened at his denial.

'I know exactly what you're thinking, Cesare,' Wolf muttered, so that only the other man could hear.

And Marco, of course; but at only fifteen months old, and not yet able to understand his father's sense of humour, he wasn't the problem Cesare was.

'Do you?' Cesare replied, half under his breath.

'Yes,' Wolf hissed back. 'And you're wrong. Completely wrong.'

'I am? But Angelica is a very beautiful woman—do you not agree?' Cesare commented, although his indulgent eyes rested on Robin rather than Angel.

'Very,' Wolf acknowledged hardly.

'And?' Cesare challenged softly.

'And nothing,' Wolf growled.

'Nothing?' Cesare turned to him with raised dark brows. 'Then you have my sincere sympathies.'

'And just what is *that* supposed to mean?' Wolf frowned his irritation.

Cesare shrugged. 'You are obviously losing your touch, cousin.'

Wolf's mouth tightened with irritation. He knew that Cesare was enjoying himself. At Wolf's expense!

'Let's just forget about my touch, shall we?' he rejoined. 'And if anyone asks, you and I are in the process of settling a business deal together.'

His cousin's brows rose higher. 'We are…?'

'We are,' Wolf confirmed.

'Who is going to ask?' Cesare enquired with deceptive mildness.

'Just do it, Cesare!' Wolf ordered.

'If you say so,' Cesare accepted. 'I believe I will go and join the ladies now.'

Leaving Wolf with no choice but to stand and watch as Cesare strolled over to join his wife and Angel.

Leaving Wolf with the uncomfortable feeling that Cesare knew exactly what had taken place between Wolf and Angel this last week…

Angelica had been totally unaware of the conversation between Wolf and Cesare as the two men had stood across the room beside the fireplace; her attention had been centred totally on the beautiful baby she held in her arms.

As if aware of her scrutiny, the baby lifted her

lashes and her huge unfocusing eyes seemed to look up at Angelica—eyes so dark a blue that they appeared almost navy, and would probably eventually become the same unusual violet colour as her mother's.

'I think I must be boring her,' Angelica said indulgently as the baby gave a tired yawn before settling back to sleep, one star-shaped hand now lying on top of the shawl.

'Not at all.' Robin chuckled as she moved to touch that tiny hand. 'You just aren't Cesare. Even at only ten days old, Carla Stephanie already knows how to charm her father and twist him around her beautiful little finger!' she confided ruefully at Angelica's questioning glance.

Carla Stephanie, Angelica noted. Carla had to be in honour of Wolf's real name—Carlo—and Stephanie because of Stephen? It seemed like a good assumption, considering how close Robin and Cesare obviously were to the two men.

'You exaggerate, Robin,' Cesare drawled as he joined them, his expression softening to one of total adoration as the baby opened her eyes just at the sound of her father's voice.

'You see,' Robin said.

Angelica did see. It also became apparent, as the three of them talked together during the next couple of minutes, that Cesare Gambrelli might be charmed by his daughter, but he absolutely worshipped his wife. Cesare, at least, did not consider it a family curse to have fallen so deeply in love with Robin.

Unlike Wolf, who had made it clear that he had no intention of falling in love with *anyone*. Least of all Angelica.

'Robin, I believe it is time that we left Stephen to rest now,' Cesare Gambrelli announced ten minutes later. 'We will come back later in the week,' he promised the older man as he bent down to take the baby from Stephen's arms. 'I expect we will see you at the house later on today, Wolf…?' he prompted lightly as he straightened.

Confirming for Angelica that Wolf *hadn't* just made up business dealings with his cousin in order to get away from here. From her. Something she had definitely suspected him of doing earlier, when he'd made that his excuse for needing to leave.

But why should Wolf need to make up an excuse to leave? He had fulfilled his obligations, hadn't he? Both to Stephen and to her?

'I think I *will* go and rest now—if you don't mind?' Stephen said tiredly, once the other couple had left with their two children. 'Will you have already left when I get up, Wolf?' he asked as he stood up.

'Probably,' the younger man confirmed abruptly.

Definitely, Angelica was sure, knowing from this morning that Wolf had no desire to spend any more time alone in her company. She stood slightly removed from the two men as Stephen once more expressed his thanks to Wolf.

The Count was standing beside the fireplace, his expression one of complete detachment, when Angelica returned from seeing Stephen settled in his bedroom. The friendly atmosphere that had been in the room while Cesare and Robin were here with the children had now turned to an icy chill, despite the fact that the sun still shone in through the windows.

Angelica raised her chin, determined. 'Please don't let me keep you if you want to go upstairs and pack your things…?'

She was dismissing him again, Wolf recognised with irritation. She was making it obvious that she didn't consider they had anything left to say to each other.

His mouth tightened. 'There really isn't that much to pack.'

She shrugged. 'Nevertheless, I'm sure you must be eager to be on your way.'

Desperate, yes. Eager, no.

Robin and Cesare's visit had only reminded Wolf of what he already knew—when a Gambrelli man loved, he seemed to give his very soul, not just his heart.

Not that Cesare didn't seem more than happy with his life the way it was now. He just wasn't the same man Wolf had known before he'd met Robin.

Until that time Cesare had been as much the carefree bachelor as Wolf and his brother Luc— the three of them often going out on the town together as they laughingly dismissed the very idea of falling in love.

But Cesare was happier now than Wolf had ever seen him, a traitorous voice murmured inside his head.

Happy, yes. Free, no.

But was that freedom so important?

Yes, damn it!

Wolf gave a terse inclination of his head. 'I am, yes,' he confirmed tautly. 'You must, of course, contact me should any problems arise concerning Stephen's health—'

'They won't,' Angel assured him tightly.

Wolf frowned. 'You can't be sure of that.'

Angelica might not be sure of it—but what she was very sure of was that Wolf was the last person she was going to contact if there should be any sort of setback in Stephen's condition.

'Peter Soames seems very confident that there will be no complications,' she insisted, wishing Wolf would just go.

Before she broke down and made a complete idiot of herself!

It was absolute hell to be standing here talking to Wolf so coolly, appearing so unconcerned, after the intimacies they had shared the night before. After her acknowledgment to herself that she was deeply in love with him!

It hadn't helped that he had looked so right earlier, holding young Marco in his arms; the family similarity had been enough—apart from the blond of Wolf's hair—that Marco could have been Wolf's son.

A son with her dark hair and Wolf's startling good looks...

Something that was never, ever, going to happen.

Despite their conversation earlier, it would be too much to hope that she had conceived Wolf's child last night.

To *hope?* she echoed to herself in surprise.

It would be a disaster if Wolf was made to come

back into her life simply because she was expecting his baby!

No, she felt confident that would never happen. No matter that the old wives' tale said that it only took the once, it very often didn't. And she knew inside herself that this time it hadn't.

No, this was definitely goodbye between herself and Wolf…

She swallowed hard. 'I'll leave you to get on, then,' she said, before turning away.

But she hadn't taken two steps towards the door before her arm was firmly grasped and Wolf swung her back to face him, his expression dark. His eyes narrowed as he looked down at her, his mouth a thin line and his jaw tightly clenched.

'Yes…?' She looked up at him quizzically.

A nerve pulsed in his jaw, and his dark eyes were glittering dangerously. 'This is for the best— you do see that?' he finally bit out harshly.

Her eyes widened. 'I have no idea what you're talking about.' She gave a shake of her head.

'Don't play games with me, Angel,' he responded impatiently, the grasp of his fingers burning through the thin material of her blouse. 'I cannot, in honour, stay here and continue with our affair now that Stephen has returned home—'

'How dare you?' she gasped with breathless

anger. 'Let go of me, Wolf!' she instructed furiously, and she struggled to shake off his hold on her arm.

Affair!

He had called what had between them last night an *affair!*

An affair just like all the other relationships he had ever had in his life. Just like with all the other women he had ever had in his life.

But wasn't that what she was to Wolf? Oh, it might be a little more complicated because she happened to be the daughter of his good friend, but besides that there was no difference between her and every other woman Wolf had ever known.

'I—said—let—go!' she repeated fiercely, digging her nails into his fingers when he still made no effort to release her.

Wolf relaxed his grip on her arm when he felt the painful sting of her nails in his flesh, knowing she had drawn blood as he felt it flowing down his hand. 'I have hurt you—'

'No!' Angel cried. 'I've hurt you,' she pointed out woodenly, and she looked down to where blood was running unchecked down his hand. 'I suggest you go and get something put on that,' she advised shortly. 'I would hate to leave any lasting mark on you!'

Wolf looked at her wordlessly for several long

seconds. '*I* have hurt *you*,' he finally insisted evenly, knowing that Angel wouldn't have reacted in the way she just had if he hadn't wounded her emotionally; even during the height of their passion the previous night she hadn't drawn blood.

She returned his gaze unblinkingly. 'I would have to care for you in order for you to have succeeded in doing that, Wolf,' she told him coldly. 'And the simple truth of the matter is that you're just a very accomplished lover.'

Wolf drew in a harsh breath at her deliberately insulting tone. 'That is what I was to you? An accomplished lover?' he repeated in a steely voice.

'Of course,' Angel answered him levelly.

It was what he had wanted to hear, wasn't it? What he had hoped? What he had needed to hear so that he could leave here with a free conscience where Angel was concerned?

It was one thing to want that. Quite another to have Angel coolly confirm that was all he had been to her!

He drew himself up to his full height of six foot three, every inch the Sicilian Count as he gave her a formal bow. 'I hope that Stephen's health continues to improve.'

'Thank you,' she accepted politely.

'Then this is goodbye,' Wolf added softly.

'Goodbye—yes,' she echoed frostily.

Angelica was glad that Wolf didn't glance back, that he closed the door behind him as he left—it would have been the height of humiliation for him to have turned and seen the hot tears she was unable to stop from tracking down her cheeks as she watched the man she loved walk out of her life.

For ever.

CHAPTER THIRTEEN

'IF YOU'RE going to start throwing things, could you pick something a little less valuable than that Ming vase you're currently holding?' Stephen requested teasingly.

Angelica glanced down at her hands, having not even been aware until that moment that she was holding a vase. A Ming vase.

She placed it carefully back on the pedestal she must have removed it from, before turning back to face Stephen as he lay on the couch near the window, enjoying the last of the sun's warm rays. The two of them had had dinner together a short time ago before retiring to the drawing room.

'I was just looking at it, that's all,' she dismissed lightly, as she clenched her hands together behind her back.

Wolf had left the house some time during the afternoon—Angelica wasn't exactly sure when. She only knew that he had gone by the time she'd come downstairs from her bedroom a couple of hours ago in order to join Stephen for dinner.

A light dinner: salmon, salad and new potatoes. But a dinner Angelica still hadn't been able to eat, having had absolutely no appetite. In fact, she'd had a sick feeling lodged in her chest all afternoon and evening.

But it wasn't a physical sickness, she knew; it had more to do with the pain of Wolf's leaving…

'Why on earth should you think I want to start throwing things?' she enquired.

Stephen grimaced. 'Possibly for the same reason that so far, during your prowling around the room, you've picked up a china shepherdess, a glass paperweight, a letter-opener, and now the Ming vase,' he came back dryly.

Had she? If so, she hadn't been aware of it.

'In fact,' Stephen continued in that same droll tone, 'I was a little apprehensive when you picked up the letter-opener! Tell me, Angel,' he went on, 'whose back were you considering sticking it into when you weighed it in your hand?'

She blinked, still having had no idea she had done any of the things Stephen said she had.

'I sincerely hope you haven't made the mistake, Angel,' Stephen added, 'of jumping to conclusions where a particular friend of mine is concerned…?'

'I have no idea what you're talking about,' she said, even as she felt the heat of colour in her cheeks.

He was referring to Wolf, of course; until today she hadn't really known any of Stephen's other friends!

And she had made no conclusions about Wolf that he hadn't totally confirmed with his own words and actions.

'Don't you?' Stephen replied mildly. 'Come and sit down for a few minutes, Angel.' He patted the sofa beside him.

Angelica crossed the room reluctantly, not wanting to have this conversation—not wanting to talk about Wolf at all.

It was bad enough that she couldn't stop thinking about him!

'Better.' Stephen nodded his satisfaction as she sat down next to him. 'Now—'

'I really don't want to talk about Wolf!' Angelica burst out anxiously.

Stephen raised his brows. 'I don't remember mentioning Wolf…'

Angelica swallowed hard, blinking back sudden tears. 'We both know Wolf's the friend you're referring to,' she said, bowing her head.

Stephen took one of her hands in his. 'Darling, the night after my operation I was a little woozy from the anaesthetic and the painkillers they had given me, but I wasn't deaf,' he told her gently.

The colour in her cheeks actually burned as she recalled being in the adjoining room with Wolf that night, lying in his arms, him making love to her, her cries and moans as Wolf pleasured her.

'Oh.' She couldn't even look at Stephen as she remembered all those things.

'Neither am I blind or insensitive,' he continued. 'The two of you have been so polite to each other this last week, so restrained whenever you've been together, but even that had changed today. Something happened between the two of you last night—no, I don't want to know what,' he assured her as she gave an embarrassed gasp. 'It's none of my damned business.' Though his gruff tone implied the opposite. 'You're a big girl, and Wolf is certainly a grown man. What I'm trying to say, Angel…' his voice softened '…is don't make the mistake of thinking that Wolf is me.'

She looked at him sharply. 'I don't—'

'That Wolf is *like* me,' Stephen enlarged. 'I married Grace because I loved her. And she loved me. But after all her miscarriages she didn't want a physical relationship—I offered to have a vasectomy, but by that time it wasn't pregnancy she feared, it was the whole marital bed thing,' he said heavily. 'We could have divorced, of course.' He sighed. 'But despite everything, no matter that we no longer had a physical relationship, or how our marriage may have appeared to other people, Grace and I still loved each other. I still love her,' he finished quietly.

Angelica swallowed hard again, not able to understand the relationship Stephen was describing, but knowing that it wasn't for her to judge the couple's relationship. The fact that she had fallen in love with Wolf was proof of that!

'Of course I ended up having affairs,' Stephen admitted. 'Your mother has the distinction of being the first of them, I'm afraid. Maybe things would have been different if Kathleen had told me she was pregnant. Maybe I would have—'

'Don't.' Angelica squeezed his hand. 'My mother and Neil are very happy together. I have twin sisters. None of that would have happened if she had told you of her pregnancy.'

'No,' he agreed. 'And it wouldn't have stopped me loving Grace, either.'

'I still don't understand what any of this has to do with Wolf,' Angelica ventured.

Stephen brightened as he smiled affectionately. 'It has to do with it because you're in love with Wolf.'

'No—'

'Oh, yes,' he went on confidently. 'And he's in love with you.'

'Most definitely no,' Angelica contradicted. 'He has some weird idea that the Gambrelli men are cursed when they fall in love—'

'Did Cesare look cursed to you?' Stephen chuckled.

'No, of course not!' she exclaimed, knowing that Cesare Gambrelli was enjoying every moment of his life with Robin. 'But I'm not the one who needs convincing! Anyway, I can't imagine why we're even having this conversation.' She stood up restlessly. 'You can't possibly want me to become involved with a man like Wolf Gambrelli!'

'I told you not to judge Wolf by my own behaviour over the last thirty years—'

'What about his *own* behaviour—?'

'No, Angel, not even by that,' Stephen insisted firmly. 'Wolf isn't a married man. He has been free to behave exactly as he chooses. But I have no doubts whatsoever that all of that will change once he meets the love of his life.'

'He doesn't *want* to meet the love of his life,' she said flatly.

'Angel, why do you think I brought the two of you together?'

Angelica turned back sharply to look at Stephen, her frown deepening as she saw the deceptively innocent expression on her father's face. 'You can't be serious!' Stephen *couldn't* have planned all this. Couldn't have wanted her and Wolf to fall in love all along. Could he…?

'Oh, I'm very serious,' Stephen said with satisfaction. 'I already think of Wolf as a son. I know him to be an honourable man—a man I respect. There isn't another man on this earth I would trust with the precious gift of my daughter.'

'But how can you feel that way?' she gasped. 'He changes his women as often as he changes his socks!'

'Or his silk sheets?' Stephen joked. 'Don't believe everything you read in the newspapers, Angel.' He gave a rueful shake of his head.

Wolf had once said the same thing to her…

'There have been women in Wolf's life, yes,' Stephen continued. 'But nowhere near the amount the gutter press would have you believe. And why shouldn't there have been women?' he reasoned. 'He's thirty-six years old and, unlike me, Wolf has never married—has never even pretended to make that sort of commitment to any woman.'

'Exactly—'

'That doesn't mean he isn't going to,' her father insisted.

'Doesn't the fact that Wolf left here at the first opportunity prove that he *isn't* in love with me?' Angelica came back, just as insistently.

Stephen shook his head. 'It proves that, like most men, Wolf is running scared even at the thought of surrendering his heart to you. But give him time, Angel,' Stephen advised. 'Let him go away and think about things for a while. Do you think you can do that?'

'What I think doesn't come into it.' Angelica was a little stunned still at the thought of Stephen's machinations. 'And I very much doubt that your friend Wolf would thank you—any more than I do, I might add!—if he knew exactly of your matchmaking this last couple of weeks!'

Stephen gave an unrepentant smile. 'I'm not asking either of you to thank me—I just want half a dozen grandchildren I can bounce on my knee!'

'Not with me as their mother and Wolf as their father, you won't,' Angelica retorted with certainty.

'We'll see,' Stephen replied enigmatically. 'In the meantime, I think it's time I went to bed.' He stood up, with her help. 'I don't suppose it will do any good for me to wish you a good night…?'

No, it wouldn't. Apart from the fact that she felt

Wolf's absence from the house too keenly to even attempt to go to sleep, this last conversation with Stephen had given her far too much to think about for her to be able to relax enough to even contemplate the idea of going to bed yet.

Wolf had no idea what he was doing, standing outside Stephen's town house ringing the doorbell at one o'clock in the morning.

But then, he hadn't had any idea of what he was doing all day—so why should now be any different?

Coming back here at this time of the night had to be the height of the madness that had held him in its grip all day.

That would probably continue to hold him in its grip for the rest of his life!

He only hoped that Holmes was still awake to answer his ring on the doorbell. And that Angel wouldn't have him thrown out of the house the moment she was woken and told that he was downstairs, demanding to see her!

Not that he intended letting himself be thrown out; whether she wanted to hear them or not, he had some things he needed to say to Angel. And he couldn't wait until the morning to say them.

All his carefully rehearsed explanations to Holmes for this late-night visit disappeared the moment the door opened and he saw Angel standing there instead of the butler, a dim light in the hallway behind her the only illumination.

She stared at him wordlessly for several long seconds before speaking. 'What are you doing here?' she asked.

She looked like moonlight and shadow, her dark hair loose about her shoulders above an equally dark dress, her bare arms and legs shimmering creamily in the low lighting.

He took a deep, sustaining breath. 'I realise how late it is—'

'Do you?' she challenged guardedly.

Of course he did, damn it. Did she think he was enjoying this?

Calm down, Wolf, he instantly cautioned himself. Having made the decision to come here and speak to her—having been *compelled* to come here and speak to her—he had no intention of being turned away without even stepping over the doorstep.

'Can I come in?' he prompted huskily.

Angelica had been sitting alone in the darkened sitting room just thinking when she'd heard the doorbell ring, and had quickly moved to answer it before any of the household staff were disturbed. She had been completely stunned to look through the door's peephole and see Wolf standing outside.

She was still stunned—had no idea what he could be doing here at one o'clock in the morning, when ordinarily everyone in the house would be fast asleep in bed.

The fact that she wasn't was due entirely to her own disturbed thoughts about this man!

'Angel?' he pressed.

She blinked. 'Isn't it a little late for a social call?' she observed dryly, still standing firmly in the doorway.

Wolf's mouth tightened. 'I'm feeling decidedly *un*social at this moment!'

He didn't exactly look in an affable mood, Angelica conceded; his hair was ruffled, as if he had been running his fingers through it, his shirt and denims were creased, and his expression was grim.

'Oh, to hell with this!' he muttered, before pushing past her and striding forcefully into the hallway.

Angelica slowly closed and locked the door behind him, then turned and watched him go into the drawing room, following at a more leisurely pace. She was unsure of exactly what Wolf's late-night visit meant, but was aware that a tiny spark of hope had ignited deep inside her...

'Leave it,' Wolf instructed harshly, as she would

have turned on the lights, and went to stand in front of the window, hands behind his back.

She gave a dismissive shrug as she moved further into the room. 'What are you doing here, Wolf?' she repeated.

Good question, he allowed. The simple truth was that he was here because *she* was here. Because he didn't want to be anywhere Angel wasn't.

He drew in a sharp breath. 'Are you absolutely certain you can't be pregnant from our time together last night?'

She blinked. 'You came back here at one o'clock in the morning to ask me that?' she said incredulously.

No, of course he hadn't come back here just to ask her that!

But it seemed as good a place as any to start this conversation...

'Are you certain?' he repeated insistently.

'No, of course not. But—'

'Would you like to be?'

She moved restlessly. 'Wolf—'

'Do you want children, Angel?' Wolf compelled. 'I know you refused to give up your career or your apartment to come and live with Stephen, so perhaps—'

'Wolf, Stephen is my father, not my husband,' she pointed out to him reasoningly.

'So you do want children?' he pushed.

'Well, of course I want children,' she confirmed. 'At some time. With a man I love and want to spend the rest of my life with.' She looked puzzled. 'But I don't see—'

'Have you found him?' Wolf interrupted. 'I never asked.' Hadn't wanted to know! 'Is there someone in your life right now, Angel?'

This had to rank as the weirdest conversation she had ever had in her life, Angelica decided, slightly dazed. And the fact that it was with Wolf, of all people, was making it even stranger...

And how did she answer his question? With the truth: *You're in my life right now*. That he always would be. That she loved him beyond reason or doubt.

Because that was the knowledge she had once again confirmed to herself as she'd sat alone in the sitting room in the steadily increasing darkness after Stephen had gone to bed. That what she felt for Wolf wasn't some transient emotion, an infatuation based on their physical compatibility; she loved him, deeply, irrevocably, and she always would.

'There *is* someone,' Wolf bit out harshly at her continued silence. 'Do you love him, Angel?'

'Oh, yes,' she admitted. 'I love him very much.'

Wolf felt as if all the breath had been knocked from his body—as if Angel had plunged a knife into his heart.

He frowned darkly. 'How can you say that after we shared a bed last night?'

'Only half the night,' she corrected softly. 'You left well before morning. And, to add insult to injury, you've behaved like a stranger towards me all day.'

'You are missing the point completely,' he came back impatiently. 'How could you have shared a bed with me, made love with me, given yourself, opened yourself to me in the way that you did, if you are in love with another man?' he challenged, with an arrogant lift of his chin.

He was the one missing the point if he couldn't see, didn't know the answer to those questions...

Angelica stared across at him, knowing she could prevaricate—lie, even. That she could hold onto her pride and let him just walk out of here without ever telling him that *he* was the man she loved, the man with whom she wanted to spend the rest of her life, wanted to have children with—beautiful Gambrelli children, like Marco and Carla.

She could.

But did she want to?

Wolf had to have come here at one o'clock in

the morning for more than questioning her further as to whether or not she could be pregnant after last night. If, for pride's sake, she avoided giving him an honest answer now, then she might never learn what that reason was…

She moistened her lips, her eyes widening slightly when she saw Wolf's eyes glitter hungrily as his gaze followed the movement. His jaw tightened as she prolonged the movement, deliberately running the tip of her tongue slowly over first her bottom lip and then her top one.

She heard as his breath caught in his throat, watched as the moonlight cast a shadow over the hard contours of his body; his shoulders were tensed, his hands clenched at his sides, his legs and thighs taut.

Yes, Wolf had come here for more than to ask her ridiculous questions. He wanted her. No matter how much he might guard his emotions, his heart, physically he wanted her again—very much.

It was a start, wasn't it…?

If admitting that *he* was the man she loved didn't frighten him off completely!

Because she wouldn't play games—wouldn't even try to pretend that she could continue a physical relationship with him without loving him when she already did love him!

'I couldn't,' she confirmed, her gaze meeting his unflinchingly.

Wolf blinked, scowling. 'But that is exactly what you did...'

'No,' Angelica contradicted, her gaze continuing to meet his steadily. 'You're right, Wolf. I couldn't have shared a bed with you last night, made love with you, given myself to you, opened myself to you, if I was in love with another man.'

Wolf continued to look at her for several stunned seconds—and then the truth of what she'd said hit him in the chest with the force of a blow, knocking the air from his body, rendering him temporarily speechless.

He was the man Angel loved and wanted to spend the rest of her life with...?

He crossed the room in three powerful strides before reaching out to clasp her arms, looking down at her intently. His arms moved about the slenderness of her waist and he lowered his head to claim her mouth with his. Gently. Searchingly. Seeking. Seeking love.

He found it. In her unreserved response to his kiss. In the slight fluttering of her hands against his chest before they moved up over his shoulders and she pressed her body against his. In the hard swell of her breasts, their tips roused and yearning.

In the heated curve of her thighs as she allowed him to mould her against him, his own hardness leaping at the intimacy.

He broke the kiss, moving his lips caressingly over the determined line of her jaw, the softness of her cheek, and then down the creamy column of her throat, his tongue seeking out the dark hollows at his base.

'I love you, Angel,' he breathed hotly against her skin. 'I love you so much that I ache! Will you marry me?'

He felt her stiffen in his arms even as she drew back slightly to look up at him, those misty grey eyes dark with confusion.

'You love me and want to marry me…?' she breathed huskily.

Wolf smiled slightly. 'You forgot to say so much that I ache,' he murmured self-derisively. 'I left here earlier today with the intention of getting as far away from you as I possibly could—'

'I'd already guessed that.'

'Hmm.' He nodded wryly. 'I got as far as Cesare and Robin's!' He sighed. 'I spent two torturous hours watching the two of them together—with them, and yet totally excluded from the love they share. They were bathing their children and putting them to bed, and all the time I knew that

I wanted my own children to play with. Your children. *Our* children,' he confirmed. 'God, Angel, I've been such a fool all these years. Such a complete and utter idiot. Loving another person, loving *you*, doesn't take away from me, make me less. It's fighting the emotion, refusing to acknowledge it, even trying to run away from it, that does that. Angel, please say you'll marry me and save me from going back to the loveless, lonely life I've led until now!'

Angelica couldn't believe that Wolf, of all people, was saying these things to her!

That he loved her. Wanted to marry her. Wanted to be the father of her children.

She reached to touch his cheek as she looked up into his eyes—those dark, melting eyes that glowed with love. For her.

She swallowed hard. 'Before I answer, I think you should know that Stephen told me earlier this evening that this is what he wanted to happen—what he planned deliberately, calculatedly, when he brought the two of us together,' she revealed.

'I'll be grateful to him for fathering you, for giving you to me, until the day I die,' Wolf vowed forcefully. 'Say you'll marry me, Angel. Say it before I go totally insane!' he urged.

'Oh, yes, Wolf,' she breathed glowingly. 'Yes, yes, *yes!*'

His mouth claimed hers in a devouring kiss that left them both breathless and shaking. Wolf was finally the one to draw back. 'I should go now,' he said. 'I don't think it's a good way to start our engagement, our life together,' he added with satisfaction, 'by having Stephen find the two of us in your bed tomorrow morning!'

Angelica laughed, so happy she felt as if she were going to burst, to shatter into a million pieces. Wolf loved her. Wanted to marry her. She was going to spend the rest of her life with him. Not with the womanising playboy she had accused him of being, but with a cursed Gambrelli—a man who loved totally, constantly, for the whole of his life…

'I don't think he would mind,' she said. 'In fact, he gave me the distinct impression earlier that the sooner the two of us get started on producing his first grandchild the better he will like it!'

Wolf's eyes darkened as he looked down at her, already knowing that he would still want her, still desire her, as her body grew ripe with their child.

He had fought against loving this beautiful woman. Had fought against loving *any* woman. Had believed that loving was a curse.

And instead it was a blessing.

Angel's love for him, and his for her, was a blessing he would want, would value, for the rest of his life.

His arms tightened about her. 'I have no idea what I have done to deserve you,' he groaned huskily. 'But I want you to know that I will love you for the rest of our lives.'

Angelica already knew that. She had absolutely no doubts that what Wolf had always thought of as the Gambrelli Curse was actually the constancy and fulfilment of a love that guided and structured the whole of their lives, and that once committed to that love the Gambrelli men would nurture and protect it above everything and everyone else.

It was the love she had always wanted, and she knew that with Wolf it was a love that would last for a lifetime.

CHAPTER FOURTEEN

'Do YOU think I should warn him?' Wolf asked Angelica six weeks later, as the two of them slowly danced together at their wedding reception.

'Warn who?' Angelica queried, laughing softly as she turned to follow Wolf's gaze across to where his brother Luc was dancing with her mother.

At thirty-four years of age, with hair the colour of molasses and those dark, dark eyes, Luc was another lethally attractive Gambrelli man. Something borne out by the fact that none of the single women in the room—and none of the married ones either!—could take their eyes off him!

They were all here—the Gambrellis, the Harpers and Stephen.

The wish Angelica had nurtured that Stephen, her mother and Neil might one day meet as friends had come true.

In fact, it had been the most wonderful day of her life.

Her family—her mother and Neil and her twin sisters—had all stayed at Stephen's house the night before, so that her mother and her sisters—her two bridesmaids—could help her dress for the wedding this morning.

She had walked down the flower-garlanded aisle on the arms of both her father and her stepfather, to be given by them to the man waiting for her at the altar. To Wolf. The man she loved to distraction.

If anything, their love for each other had deepened in the last six weeks. Wolf was un-ashamedly open about his feelings for her, as she was in her love for him.

'No, I don't think you should warn Luc,' she answered her husband now.

Wolf glanced across at his younger brother, knowing that not even Kathleen, a woman happily married for the last twenty-one years, would remain immune to his easy charm. That no woman was safe against Luc's lethal seductiveness.

'No, perhaps it will be better to let him discover the true fate of a Gambrelli man—the joy and the utter fulfilment of love—for himself,' Wolf agreed, and he turned his attention back to his wife.

His *wife*!

He could still barely believe that this beautiful woman was his. He had woken up each morning for the last six weeks pinching himself to make sure it was true, and today she had become his wife.

He loved her more than life itself—had never felt so happy. And all of that happiness was contained within Angel's beautiful, loving heart.

He intended loving and cherishing her for a lifetime.

'I have a wedding gift for you,' Angel told him shyly.

'But I am already wearing the cufflinks you gave me.' Wolf frowned his puzzlement.

And she was wearing the beautiful diamond pendant that Wolf had presented to her the evening before, the tear-shaped jewel nestling warmly in the swell of her breasts.

'I have another gift for you,' she assured him throatily, before reaching up to whisper in his ear.

Wolf's arm tightened about her waist, his eyes glittering as he looked down at her. 'You're sure?' he checked gruffly, wonderingly.

'Absolutely,' she assured him, smiling.

'I—You—God, Angel, you take my breath away!' he acknowledged raggedly, and he looked down at her adoringly. 'I never dreamed—never knew—that loving someone, loving *you*, could fill me so completely.' His head lowered and he kissed her gently, achingly, his eyes once more glowing as he raised his head. 'We have to tell Stephen!' he told her excitedly, and he grasped her hand and began striding through the throng of dancing guests to cross the room to where Stephen and Neil sat in conversation.

Angel laughed softly, exultantly, loving Wolf with that same overwhelming completion with which she knew that she carried their son or daughter deep inside her.

The first of those dozen children that Wolf had told her would be the lasting proof of the love of this Gambrelli man…

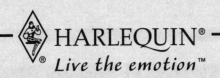
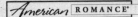

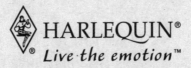

HARLEQUIN®
INTRIGUE®

BREATHTAKING ROMANTIC SUSPENSE

Shared dangers and passions lead to electrifying romance and heart-stopping suspense!

Every month, you'll meet six new heroes who are guaranteed to make your spine tingle and your pulse pound. With them you'll enter into the exciting world of Harlequin Intrigue— where your life is on the line and so is your heart!

THAT'S INTRIGUE—
ROMANTIC SUSPENSE
AT ITS BEST!

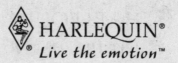

HARLEQUIN®
Live the emotion™

HARLEQUIN®

SuperRomance®

...there's more to the story!

Superromance.
A *big* satisfying read about unforgettable
characters. Each month we offer *six* very different
stories that range from family drama to adventure
and mystery, from highly emotional stories to
romantic comedies—and much more! Stories
about people you'll believe in and care about.
Stories too compelling to put down....

Our authors are among today's *best* romance
writers. You'll find familiar names and talented
newcomers. Many of them are award winners—
and you'll see why!

If you want the biggest and best
in romance fiction, you'll get it
from Superromance!

Exciting, Emotional, Unexpected...

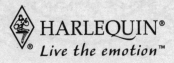

HARLEQUIN®
Live the emotion™

www.eHarlequin.com   HSDIR06

Harlequin® Historical
Historical Romantic Adventure!

*Imagine a time of chivalrous
knights and unconventional ladies,
roguish rakes and impetuous
heiresses, rugged cowboys
and spirited frontierswomen—
these rich and vivid tales will
capture your imagination!*

*Harlequin Historical . . .
they're too good to miss!*

Silhouette®

SPECIAL EDITION™

*Emotional, compelling stories that capture the intensity of
living, loving and creating a family in today's world.*

Silhouette® Desire

Modern, passionate reads that are powerful and provocative.

Silhouette® nocturne

Dramatic and sensual tales of paranormal romance.

Silhouette® Romantic SUSPENSE

Romances that are sparked by danger and fueled by passion.

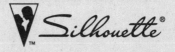